FLASHBACK

BY TERESA COLTON

All contents of this digital book are copyright 2020 to Teresa Colton.

ISBN: 9798678559593

All rights reserved: no part of this publication may be reproduced, stored in a retrieval system, or transmitted, in any form or by any means, electronic, mechanical, photocopying or otherwise, without the prior consent of the author.

Cover design by Teresa Colton.

Chapter 1

'Shannon!' I heard someone call from behind me. I pictured a runaway child whose mother was afraid they would run into the road.

'Shannon! Wait!' I carried on walking but suddenly felt someone's hand on my shoulder. I turned abruptly to see a dark haired woman of about thirty years of age looking at me, an expression of disbelief on her face.

'I can't believe it. Everyone thought you were.......dead. Where have you been for the last four years?'

Now it was my turn to look puzzled, 'I'm sorry, should I know you?'

She took a step back, the smile fading on her face, 'Of course you know me. Eve Pritchard. We were best friends at one time.'

I stared at her, taking in the small features framed by dark curls. She was wearing a floral sundress, and over her arm she carried a hessian shopping bag.

I looked away, 'I'm sorry, I don't believe we've met before, and my name's not Shannon.'

I turned to go, but she grabbed my arm, 'I don't know what you're playing at, but I'd know you anywhere. Why don't we go to the café and talk?'

I shook her hand off my arm and looked her straight in the face, 'I don't know you.' Then I walked off, leaving her standing on the pavement.

Whoever she was, she'd got it all wrong. I was Lee Filmer, twenty eight years old and resident in the small town of Barling. Or rather in Hanley Cross, one of the villages just outside the town. I had inherited the cottage from an aunt, apparently, an aunt I never knew I had, but she was by all accounts very close to my mother. And that was another thing. I don't remember my parents either. The accident had wiped out all memories of my past life, the only memories I could access were the ones made after my recovery, the earliest one being waking up in hospital, my head swathed in bandages and a doctor standing by my bedside, watching as I slowly regained consciousness.

'Welcome back,' I heard him say, 'You had us all worried for a while, but you're going to be fine. You just need to rest.'

I must have drifted away again as the next time I opened my eyes it was dark and the doctor had gone. I was conscious of a slight headache, but otherwise felt stronger. I was obviously in hospital, but how did I get there? What had happened to cause me to be hospitalised? Maybe I wasn't as well as I thought. My head was muzzy with trying to think, and nothing was coming back to me.

The door opened and a light came on, hurting my eyes till I got used to the brightness. A nurse came in carrying a small round tray with a mug on and a plate of biscuits.

'The doctor says we can remove the drip in your arm,' she said with a smile, 'I thought you might like some cocoa.'

Cocoa! Ugh! Far too sweet for me. How strange I could remember that I didn't like cocoa when I couldn't even remember my own name. It was unnerving.

'What happened to me?' my voice was weak and scratchy, 'How did I get here?'

'The doctor will be in shortly, he'll explain everything.' She removed the drip from my arm and disappeared as quickly as she had come.

I stared at the mug. There was no potted plant that I could dispose of the sickly contents in, so it would just have to stay there getting cold.

The doctor arrived, checked the monitors I was still

hooked up to, then pulled up a chair and sat by my bed.

'How are you feeling, Lee?'

Lee? The name didn't sound familiar.

I swallowed and said, 'A slight headache, but I don't remember anything. What happened to me, Dr?'

'You don't remember the accident, the car crash?'

'I don't even know who I am.'

'You were in the back seat of a vehicle driven by your father. I'm very sorry, but your parents did not survive the crash.'

I sat bolt upright, the wires from the monitors straining as I moved.

'My parents died and I can't even remember them,' I had never been so terrified. 'How do I cope with that?' I asked helplessly.

'We'll give you all the help we can,' the doctor was saying, but his words were a blur. 'Lee, do you remember anything at all?'

I sank back on the pillows, 'No. Nothing! The first thing I remember is waking up here a few hours ago. You were here.'

He nodded slowly, 'Lee, you hit your head really badly. We had to operate straight away or we would have lost you. I can't guarantee you will get your memory back. The best thing you can do is start fresh from this moment and move on. I'm not saying you should forget your parents, but if not remembering them is causing you stress, then you have to let it go.'

'Are you saying I won't get anything back, no snippets, no vague thoughts about my past?'

'Never say never, but it's not likely. All the information you need was in your handbag. It's rather battered I'm afraid, but there were documents in it giving your name, address, national insurance card, and even your passport.'

So this was it! Half a lifetime gone and nothing at all to show for it. I didn't know if I had any other family, I didn't know if I had a career, all I knew was that I didn't like cocoa! Not much for............however many years I'd been on this planet. This was truly terrifying!

But I was alive. I closed my eyes and tried to grieve for the parents I didn't know I had.

* * * * *

Reaching my car, parked in the town's main car park, all this came flooding back to me. Maybe Eve Pritchard was right after all, maybe I was Shannon in my past life. I had been encouraged to let the past go and that seemed to me the best way to go forward, concentrate on the future. You can't change the past so if its hurting you, let it go.

But suddenly that wasn't enough. I had a past and I wanted to know everything about it. And there was only one person who could possibly help me.

I had to find Eve Pritchard.

Chapter 2

The Chase/Colbourne building stood in the industrial area of Dengate, having moved there when the new high rise office blocks were constructed. The building was mostly glass fronted, making the offices light and airy, but the building itself was a modern carbuncle in the ancient town of Dengate, with its Tudor buildings, quaint tea shops and open market square. Chase/Colbourne Enterprises had begun life as an architectural firm, but had grown to such an extent, they now had their fingers in a number of pies, resulting in them becoming a multi-millionaire establishment. The company had been formed over twenty years ago by Joseph Chase, later joined by Andrew Colbourne, when their companies had merged. Andrew, being the older partner by a good twenty years, had recently taken a step back, letting his son, Mark, take the reins.

This was bitterly resented by Joseph's nephew, Christopher, who had joined the firm after leaving university with a degree in business studies, and had been Joseph's right hand man ever since.

He now walked along the cream-painted corridor on the top floor and knocked on the door of his uncle's office, opening it before Joseph had time to say 'Come in.'

Joseph was sitting at his desk surrounded by paperwork. He looked up as Chris stood in front of him, leaning forward with both hands on the desk.

'I should let Mark deal with all this,' Joseph said, 'No point in having a dog and barking yourself!'

Chris smiled wryly, 'Have you thought any more about what we discussed the other day?'

'I told you I'd bring it up at the next board meeting. I

can't foresee how they're going to react though.'

'But you will steer things in my favour.'

'They're all aware of what you do for the firm, Chris. It will be up to them to decide as a group. I don't have so much sway now. Mark's in line to be the next chairman, however long that will take, but I'll do what I can. I can't say fairer than that.'

'I'm the closest relative you've got. I've been with this firm all my working life, and I'm good at what I do. You know those last two big deals were down to me. My business acumen and loyalty must count for something!'

'Of course it does, Chris. No one's disputing you are a valuable asset to the firm, but that doesn't guarantee you a place on the board. All this has sprung up since Mark was made a partner, would you have brought it up if things had remained the same as they were before that?'

Chris stood upright, towering over his Uncle, 'Mark's an idiot! He's had neither the training or the experience that I've had. He would have lost that last deal if I hadn't stepped in and saved it. I can't believe Andrew didn't see that coming!'

'That's a matter of opinion, Chris. Andrew and I have always seen Mark as a competent leader, who always has the interest of this firm at heart. Okay, he made a mistake with the Bridger account, but realised what he'd done in time to avert a catastrophe. You were a bit quicker spotting it, but he's learnt by his mistakes. The board were happy to vote him in as a partner and subsequently their future chairman.'

'The board were brainwashed into it! Andrew's a great influence on them, and the majority went along with it. Now I'm asking you to do the same for me.'

'Chris, I can't and I won't influence the board, other than to say I'm in favour of you becoming a junior partner. Mark got his promotion on merit and you must do the same.'

Chris stared defiantly at his uncle, 'I'm good for the firm

and you know it. I know we haven't always seen eye to eye, but don't let personal feelings get in the way of your decision. Unless you want to see the company go down the drain!'

Joseph looked down at the untidy mass of papers on his desk, 'I've got work to do, Chris. This conversation is over.'

Christopher glared at his uncle for a long minute, then turned and walked out of the room, not quite slamming the door, but shutting it with a force that made the picture on the wall shake.

Joseph got up and straightened the picture, standing to look at it for a few minutes before returning to his desk. It was a portrait of his late wife. Joseph sighed, 'Oh, Isla. If only you were still here. If only.........' He couldn't go on. It was too painful.

Chapter 3

Lee

The first thing I did when I got home was to look in the phone directory to find Eve Pritchard's number.

There were two possibilities listed in the Dengate area. The first one I drew a blank, Elizabeth Pritchard was an elderly spinster living alone. She had no relatives in the area, and did not know anyone called Eve. I dialled the second number. This was answered by a man. Edward Pritchard said his wife was out, but her name was Ruth, not Eve, and like the previous call, he did not know anyone of that name.

This was going to be more difficult then I thought. Eve's number must be unlisted, or maybe she didn't have a house phone at all. Like so many people these days, she may use a mobile only. There was no directory for that, so I got the laptop out and googled her name. The two Pritchards I'd already rung came up, but still no one called Eve. She did not seem to exist. But of course that was nonsense; she had grabbed hold of my arm with a firm grip. I couldn't have imagined the whole episode, could I?

The doctor had told me I may experience one or two mild hallucinations, partly due to my head injury, partly due to the medication, but the dose had been significantly lowered recently, and I'd had very little trouble in that direction. So why would the hallucinations suddenly start up again? No, Eve Pritchard had been real. I didn't remember her from before, but I would know her immediately if I ever saw her again.

The doorbell rang, making me jump. I came out of my

reverie and went to open the door, to find Flynn standing on the step.

'You've forgotten!' he said amiably, 'The Dengate fete?'

I ran my fingers through my hair, 'I'm sorry, Flynn. I did forget. I hadn't realised what the time was.'

Short term memory loss was another thing I had to contend with, but the doctor had assured me this was only a temporary thing, and was expected to improve as time went on.

'Give me a minute to get ready,' I said to Flynn, I was now half way up the stairs heading for the bathroom where I could hopefully make myself presentable.

When I got back downstairs Flynn was in the kitchen, having just made himself a cup of coffee.

'I hope you don't mind,' he said, with a lopsided grin, 'I know how long you women take to get ready.'

'You have a vast experience of women's habits?' I returned. I could be facetious too!

I had met Flynn Wyatt a few days after moving to the Dengate area. Once again I had parked in the town's main car park, and whilst fishing in my bag for my keys, had promptly dropped them down a grid I was parked halfway across. I bent down to see them lodged on a metal bar, just far enough down inside the drain to be unreachable. 'Oh, crap!' I said aloud, hoping there was no one around to hear me.

'Can I be of assistance?'

I looked up and saw a man with the deepest blue eyes I'd ever seen. He was the original tall, dark and handsome man you read about in Mills and Boon romantic fiction.

'I've dropped my keys down this grid,' I said, stating the obvious.

I stood up, and he took my place crouching on the ground peering into the grid. He rattled the cover gently, but it was not going to come off.

He stood up, 'I can't put any more force on the grid in case I dislodge the keys and they fall down further.'

He looked around, and went to a tree growing on the other side of the car park, snapped off a straight branch and came back shedding the leaves from it as he walked.

'This might work' he said, hopefully, lowering the twig through the bars and deftly hooking it through the key ring. Slowly he raised it up level with the top of the grid, reaching into it to bring the keys back up through the bars.

I breathed a sigh of relief. 'Thank you,' I said, holding out my hand for the keys.

He palmed them, with a grin. 'I'll give them back on one condition. You have dinner with me tonight.'

I wasn't expecting that! But he had a kindly face and he had saved me a whole lot of hassle by retrieving the keys.

'That will depend,' I said, 'I never have dinner with anyone if I don't know their name.'

'Flynn Wyatt,' he said, handing me the keys, 'Do you know the Green Dragon? I've heard they do excellent meals there.'

'Lee Filmer,' I answered, 'And you're right, they do a mean steak and chips.'

'Seven o'clock then. I'll see you later, Lee Filmer.'

That was nearly a month ago, and I had seen Flynn several times since then. I had been wary of getting into a relationship as I still hadn't got a proper grip on my condition, but I explained all that to Flynn, and he seemed to understand. He laughed off my lapses of memory, and the other idiosyncrasies that I wasn't even sure were due to the accident, and I gradually relaxed in his company. He was good for me, and this was all helping me to move forward.

The coffee drunk, we set off for the fete. Dengate fete was an annual fund raising event, he informed me. Over the past few years it had raised a lot of money for the local hospital. It was held on the sports field and consisted of a number of varied events during the afternoon, a dog show, a display by some majorettes, even the local Morris dance team had turned up, and were waving handkerchiefs during a dance as we came through the main gates. Their music was lively, an accordionist, a guitarist, and someone playing a bodhran completed their little group and made you want to jig along with them. We stopped for a while to watch, along with a large group of people who had gathered around the makeshift arena. The dancers looked very colourful in their outfits but I was wary of the hooden horse and hoped he would stay on the other side of the arena! There were also a number of interesting looking stalls around the perimeter of the field, selling crafts, homemade fudge, and bric-a-brac.

There was a beer tent and a tea tent selling cakes donated by the women on the committee.

It was a scorchingly hot day in August, we were in the middle of a heatwave and a long cool drink sounded good, so we went straight to the beer tent. All the tables inside were taken, so we took our drinks outside. I felt the sting across my shoulders, which told me I was starting to burn as the sun blazed down, and I knew I was going to have two thin white stripes across my shoulders where the straps of my sundress lay. I hadn't bothered to stop and properly sun-cream myself, not wanting to keep Flynn waiting. Big mistake! Now I would have to suffer the beetroot coloured skin and the agony of the burn!

We walked slowly round the field, stopping to look at the delicate crafts on the stalls as we passed them. There were a lot of talented people about, wood turners, paper crafts and even a woman spinning yarn on an old wooden spinning wheel. But my mind was still on the woman who had approached me in the town that morning.

'Flynn,' I said, 'Have you ever heard of a woman called Eve Pritchard?'

He thought for a moment, 'Don't think so. Why, is she a friend of yours?'

'No, I'm trying to locate her. She may be able to tell me something about my past.'

'I thought you had agreed with the doctor to let that go. You'll only get disappointed again, and that's not going to help your recovery, is it?'

'I suppose not, but if I don't try I'll never know.'

'Why do you think this woman can help anyway? How do you know her?'

'I don't know her, but she thinks she knows me. She called me Shannon this morning in town. I told her that wasn't my name, and then I walked away. I wish I'd listened to her now. She's proving very difficult to track down.'

'What else did she say? Did she tell you who Shannon was?'

'No, I didn't really give her the chance. But she did say she thought Shannon was dead. What do you make of that?'

'She's a crank! You're doing so well, Lee, I wouldn't like to see you go backwards.'

Maybe he was right, but I wasn't giving up. Somehow I was going to chase up any clues that might lead to me finding out who I really was. Flynn could come along for the ride, or not.

Chapter 4

Detective Chief Inspector Frank Hutton and his family were enjoying the fete. It was rare that they got out together as a family due to Frank's job, to say he worked unsocial hours was an understatement. The older children had gone off to wander round on their own, Frank and Netta were watching the majorettes twirling their batons and marching round the display area.

'This is nice,' Netta said, 'Last year I had to wander round with the kids on my own, and Robbie was only four months old and screamed most of the time.' She looked fondly down at her sixteen-month-old, swigging orange juice from a spouted cup. No screaming this year, the child was taking in all the entertainment from the comfort of his pushchair, a parasol shielding his head from the blazing sun.

Frank smiled, remembering how Netta had so not wanted him when she first found out she was pregnant, but now nothing was too good for the dark-haired little boy.

It was a hot, humid afternoon, and Frank would have rather been at home watching the sport on the TV, but Netta had persuaded him to come to the fete. And if he was honest, he was quite enjoying it, at least until a scream suddenly rang out and he saw a woman dressed in a long tiered skirt and gypsy-style blouse rush out of the fortune teller's tent, 'Help! Someone help. There's been a murder!'

'Don't come any closer,' Frank said to Netta, before running towards the tent where the screaming woman was waving her arms around hysterically.

'I'm Detective Chief Inspector Hutton. Calm down. Let's

go somewhere quieter and you can tell me what happened.' He started to lead her into the tent, but she pulled back, 'Not in there, it's horrible!'

Frank looked round and spotted a bench, 'All right, go and wait on that bench, I'll find someone to come and look after you.'

Hutton took a peep into the tent, having got the fortune teller safely out of the way, and saw a woman sitting in a chair, her head thrown back, displaying a ligature right across her throat. Blood was streaming from the injury, which made the scene gory enough to terrify the gypsy fortune teller.

He exited the tent and called his sergeant, who he had seen earlier buying jewellery from a craft stall. Then he called the police pathologist, who wasn't at the fete, but promised to be on the scene within twenty minutes.

There was little Frank could do except determine that life was extinct, till Carsdale and the forensic team got there.

A small crowd had gathered, believing this was another event in the programme, a murder mystery game.

'Would you all move back please.' Frank raised his voice, 'There's been an incident. I'm a police officer and I want this area cleared.'

People started to move away, and DS Lang hurried towards the tent. She had been enjoying a cup of tea and a slice of homemade sponge cake when Hutton's call had come through.

'What have we got, sir?' she asked, looking at the tent. Hutton pulled aside the canvas flap that acted as a door and Stephanie peered inside. 'Nasty. Do we know who she is?'

'Not yet. I've had to stand guard to stop the vultures getting in! They think it's part of the show.'

'Well, murder mysteries are popular these days. Been to a few myself and never get it right!'

Hutton directed his gaze to the fortune teller sitting

quietly on the bench, 'She was the one who found the body. Can you see she's okay, and find out what actually happened? I'll wait here for Carsdale's lot.'

Right on cue, Hutton saw the coroner's vehicle coming through the main gates, trying not to mow down the strolling people who seemed determined not to get out of the way.

Malcolm Carsdale got out of the vehicle and approached Hutton, 'Nice place to stage a murder,' he said drily, 'Plenty of kids around to stumble over a gory body. Where's the victim, Frank?'

Huttton led him into the tent. He walked slowly round the body, his hand rubbing his chin, 'Mmm, you don't need me to tell you she's been garroted. He ran a gloved finger over the ligature, 'Could have been done with a wire or nylon thread, something off a stringed musical instrument would be my guess.'

'How long has she been dead?' was Hutton's next question.

'I'd say anything up to an hour, hour and a half at most. No longer.'

'The fortune teller went for her break at 3 o'clock and was back by about twenty past. That's when she discovered the body.'

'That certainly narrows it down. Unless she was killed somewhere else and deposited here. Know more after the autopsy.'

'Bit risky, carrying a dead body around in a field with three or four hundred spectators, I would have thought.'

'Stranger things have happened. Killers get cocky, think they are clever and can pull it off. Until one day they get complacent and slip up. But from what I've seen so far I would agree, this woman was killed right here in this chair.'

Hutton left the pathologist to do his job and returned to the field to find the area taped off and forensics scouring the ground. I'll be surprised if they find any footprints, he thought to himself, the ground had been baked to a cinder over the past couple of weeks, and should they get lucky, it could be any of the people in this field that had decided to have their palms read this afternoon.

'Inspector Hutton?' His reverie ended as he saw a portly man coming towards him, 'I am Jonathan Swinley, Chairman of the Dengate fete committee. What's all this about a murder?'

'There has been an incident, sir. I would be grateful if you would play this down and get everyone to leave the field quickly and quietly. We don't want to start a mass panic.'

'Are you saying we have to pack up? Good Lord, man, we've only been here a couple of hours! Is that really necessary?'

'The incident has resulted in a death. This field is now a crime scene. The stall holders may remain long enough to pack their things up, but they must keep to their own pitch and not wander about. Is that clear, sir?'

'As ditchwater!' Swinley stalked off, and Hutton joined Stephanie who had flagged down a passing eavesdropper and got her to fetch the fortune teller a cup of tea.

'This is Yvonne Whitmore,' Stephanie said, then to Yvonne, 'This is DCI Hutton.'

'How are you feeling now, Miss Whitmore?' Hutton asked. The woman was visibly calmer, thanks to Stephanie, who had a calming effect on people – when she wanted to.

Yvonne Whitmore looked up at him with a wry smile, 'Some fortune teller I am! Didn't see that one coming, did I! .....Sorry, inspector. Bad joke. Put it down to shock.'

'Can you tell me what happened?'

Yvonne sighed, 'I didn't want to do this clairvoyant thing, but I got roped in as no one else wanted to do it either, and they said I looked the part, and it is for charity. Anyway, I went for my break at 3 o'clock. It was hot and stuffy in that tent, and I needed a cup of tea. I was gone about fifteen minutes, then I went back to the tent. At first I thought that woman had come for a palm reading and had fallen asleep waiting for me, but then I saw the blood and that gash on her neck. I could see she was dead and I panicked and ran out of the tent. Then you came along.'

'Did you see anyone near the tent on your way back?'

'No, nobody. I'd hung a sign up saying I was on a break. So there wasn't any reason for anyone to be in this area. But there's a low fence leading to the woods behind us. I suppose they could have escaped that way.'

'We've got officers checking that out,' said Hutton, 'Miss Whitmore, do you have any idea who the unfortunate lady is?'

'She looked vaguely familiar, but no one I know. I've probably seen her around town sometime.'

'Okay, thank you, that's all for now. I'll get someone to run you home.'

'Thanks, but I'd rather walk. I don't live far from here.'

Hutton and Lang watched her walk towards the main gates to join the throngs of people already lining up to get out.

'She said she went for a cup of tea, sir,' said Stephanie, 'I was in the tea tent at that time, and I'm pretty sure that she wasn't!'

The Morris dancers were loading their instruments and costumes into their van. Most had changed back into their ordinary clothes and were ready to go home. The accordionist looked round as Hutton and Lang approached them, both holding out their warrant cards.

'Detective Chief Inspector Hutton, this is DS Lang. We'd like a quick word.'

'What's going on, inspector. We were told someone had died and the fete is over.' He was a large man with long grey hair tied back in a ponytail.

'There has been an incident which resulted in a death,

sir. Let's start with your name?'

'Tony Crossley. And this incident happened in the fortune teller's tent I'm assuming, by the activity going on over there. But I didn't go over that side of the field and I'm pretty sure none of my group did either. We tend to mostly stick together at these events.'

'Where do you leave your instruments when you're not performing?' Hutton asked.

'We keep them in the van. What has our music got to do with anything?'

'Hopefully nothing at all, Mr. Crossley. It's the guitar we're interested in. Is the owner still here?'

'He's just over there' Crossley said, nodding his head to where two men were standing talking. 'Joe! Someone wants a word!'

Joe Withington was a slight man, also with the obligatory grey ponytail, characteristic of many folk singers.

'Police' said Crossley as he approached them, 'Want a word about your guitar.'

Withington grinned, 'Haven't broken any noise pollution laws have I?' he asked, looking at Hutton and then glancing at Lang. She was a fine looking woman and no mistake, but he wouldn't want to get on the wrong side of her. She looked as if she'd eat you for breakfast if you upset her- she was way out of his league. He turned his attention back to Hutton.

'So. My guitar. What has that got to do with anything?'

'Where is it now, sir? Could we take a look?'

Withington went round to the back of the van and pulled out his guitar case, a solid looking thing which he laid on the ground, and opened it up to reveal a cherry-wood guitar lying on a black felted lining.

'Hutton bent over the case and peered in noting that all six strings were present. 'Do you carry spare strings when you go to gigs?' he asked, straightening up again.

'Of course' Withington replied, scratching his head,

'Why the interest in guitar strings?'

'It appears the victim might have been strangled with one, or something like one. Would you mind checking to see if your spares are all there?'

'Jesus!' exclaimed Withington, 'You think someone nicked one out of the van?'

'Was the van kept unlocked?' asked Hutton, noting the position of the van in comparison to where the dancing had taken place. There were other vehicles belonging to stall holders in the field, all parked several yards behind the stalls themselves. It wouldn't be difficult for someone to slip in to the van and help themselves to the strings, if they were stealthy enough.

Withington disappeared into the back of the van again and came out shaking his head. 'There was a new packet of strings in the bag, but they're not there now. Whole packet gone! Looks like you might be right, inspector.'

'And I suppose none of you saw anyone creeping around the van?' Hutton said, not at all hopeful that they would have done so.

Both men shook their heads. 'Someone must have nipped in while we were dancing,' Crossley offered, 'That's the only time the van was left unattended.'

Hutton and Lang walked back across the field to the crime scene. 'Get someone to go through the rubbish bins before they take them away, Steph. The killer only needed one string to do the job. What happened to the other five?'

'Might get some prints off the packet I suppose.' Stephanie said, looking longingly at the tea tent, and wishing she could have finished her sponge cake. The hunger pangs were kicking in, this was not the way she had planned to spend her afternoon off. The deceased woman had been helping in the tea tent, she may even have made the cake herself. Suddenly Stephanie wasn't hungry anymore.

Chapter 5

Lee

Something was happening at the far end of the field. There was a lot of police activity in and around the fortune teller's tent. Flynn had gone back to the car, which was parked in an adjacent field, to fetch his wallet which he had shoved into the glove compartment after buying petrol on the way here. This was the second time he'd left me during the afternoon, the first being to check he'd locked the car. He could have collected the wallet then, but hadn't remembered he'd left it there at the time. It seemed I wasn't the only one with memory lapses!

I wandered slowly towards the action. The crowds were surging towards the gate as there had been an announcement that there had been an accident and the fete was now over. I would be near the back of the line so I decided to go walk-about until the majority of the crowd had dispersed. And there was always the chance I might spot Eve Pritchard if she was here. I noticed there was now police tape sealing off the area, and what looked like a coroner's van parked just behind the tent. But then those of us who were still hanging around the area were told by a uniformed officer to move away, and there was a second announcement over the loudspeaker instructing everyone to leave the field. People were crowding towards the main gates, but no one seemed in a hurry to leave. Everyone wanted a piece of the action, everyone wanted to be the first to know what was going on. I walked back towards them, watching the slow exodus, thinking a position near the gate, but not actually in the line, would be the best position to spot Eve Pritchard if she was here. There was only one way out, so unless you wanted to leap over the fence at the rear of the field and walk through the woods, Eve would have to pass by me, that is unless she had been one of the first to exit while I'd been occupied at the other end of the field.

I glanced at my watch, Flynn was taking his time. It wasn't that far to walk to the car.

I scanned the faces of every woman that went through the gates, but Eve Pritchard was not among them.

The sun was lower in the sky now, but just as hot. I needed a cold drink and the shower I had not had time for, due to Flynn's arrival on my doorstep, and was about to give up and join the queue when I saw him pushing his way through the crowd, trying to get to me.

'Where have you been?' I said accusingly.

He pulled his wallet out of his back trouser pocket, 'To get this. Then on the way back I met someone I knew who told me there had been a murder. Have you heard anything?'

'The official announcement said there had been an accident, but people are talking. That looks like a coroner's van' I said, pointing to the black vehicle that had ploughed through the crowd earlier, scattering people in all directions, 'They don't normally turn up for accidents unless it's fatal.'

'Well, no point in hanging about here,' Flynn said, looking for a gap in mass of people to squeeze through.

'No, not yet,' I said, pulling him back, 'I haven't given up looking for Eve Pritchard. If she's here she'll have to come through these gates. It's the only way out.'

Flynn sighed and gave me a look that you would give when indulging a petulant child, but he patiently stayed with me until the last person had left the field.

Eve Pritchard was not among them.

Chapter 6

Frank and Stephanie sat on the bench Yvonne Whitmore had recently vacated, watching the officials shepherding people out of the field. Frank caught sight of Netta pushing Robbie over the rough ground. She had been joined by Jack and Jessie, and also their niece, Michelle. How Michelle had matured this last year, he thought. She had become a confident, able young woman, despite the trauma she had experienced two years previously, when she had narrowly escaped being murdered, and by a girl who she had believed to be her best friend.

The family had been worried that the incident would have some unsavoury repercussions, but Michelle was a lot stronger than that, and had managed to put it all behind her and move on. Now at university, she was studying law, hoping to become a lawyer. Frank's own children could do worse than follow their cousin's example.

Back in the tent, they found Carsdale finishing up. The body had been removed to the morgue and the forensic team were still searching the area.

'Ah, Frank,' Carsdale said as the officers entered the tent, 'I've got a name for you. Found her handbag under the table. Driving license says she's a Mrs Eve Pritchard. Lives at no.4, Willow Court, Barling Halt.'

'It's that group of houses right in the centre of the village,' Stephanie said.

'Anything else you can tell us?' Hutton asked.

'Freshly broken finger nail. Probably incurred as she tried to fight off her attacker. She was attacked from behind, probably by someone she knew. The chair was facing straight onto the desk, and the position of the body suggests she felt comfortable letting this person wander back behind her. Anything else you'll have to wait for till after the autopsy. Funny thing, fortune telling, I once had an aunt who was told by a clairvoyant she would become big in the field of athletics. Fell and broke two major bones in her leg in her first big race. Never ran again!'

* * * * *

'This is my least favourite part of the job' Stephanie mused as they walked up the path to the Pritchard's front door and rang the bell. The door was answered by a man with a small child balanced on his hip and another clinging to one of his legs.

'Mr Pritchard? I am Detective Chief Inspector Hutton from Barling CID, this is Sergeant Lang. Might we come in?'

Darren Pritchard froze, 'What's happened? Is it Eve?'

'It would be better if we could talk inside,' Hutton said gently.

Darren bent down to detach the little girl from his leg, and stood aside to allow the officers to enter. He led them into a sitting room covered in toys. A playpen stood under the window and he lowered the baby into it.

'Shall we all sit down?' Stephanie said, easing herself onto the large sofa.

'Mr Pritchard,' Hutton began, 'There's been an incident at the fete this afternoon. I'm sorry to tell you your wife was attacked, and unfortunately didn't survive.'

Hutton let this information sink in for a moment. Darren sat staring into space. Then he looked at Hutton, 'Eve's dead? How did it happen?'

'She was strangled. She was found in the fortune teller's tent, we believe she went there for a reading, but the fortune teller was on a break. We think Eve decided to wait for her.'

'Eve was into all that,' Darren volunteered, his voice barely audible. 'She went to the spiritualist church, I didn't like it, lot of mumbo jumbo, but she thought it was all genuine.'

He looked at Hutton, 'Why would anyone want to kill her?'

'That's what we're trying to find out,' Hutton replied, 'How did your wife seem before she left for the fete? Did she appear to have anything on her mind?'

'She was just normal, looking forward to the fete. She was helping in the tea tent. Eve loves....loved getting involved with charitable events.'

'Can you think of anyone who had a grudge against her? Had she upset anyone?'

'No! Eve didn't like confrontation. She was a people person, liked everyone and everyone liked her.'

Hutton's eyes focused on a guitar propped up against the wall. 'You play?' he asked.

'I used to,' Darren said, 'I was in a band. Gave it all up when the kids came along.'

'You appear to have a string missing.'

'Jasmine did that. I shouldn't have let her touch it' Darren said, looking at his daughter. Hutton nodded thoughtfully.

The mention of his daughter brought a look of consternation to Darren's face. He was watching the child who was building something unrecognisable with some large Lego type bricks. 'The children. How am I going to tell them their mum's not coming back?'

'Do you have someone who could help you with the children? Their grandparents perhaps?' asked Stephanie.

'Both my family and Eve's live nearby. I'll let them know what's happened.'

'Why didn't you accompany your wife to the fete, Mr Pritchard. I would have thought it was something the children would have liked.'

'They're too young to take part in any of the events,

and Eve was going to be in the tea tent most of the time. We decided they'd be better off here.'

Hutton stood up and handed Darren a card. 'Call me anytime if you think of anything that might help.'

After a slight pause Darren said, 'It's probably nothing, inspector, but there was one thing that strikes me as a bit strange, though I can't see how it has any relevance to Eve being killed, but she did say she saw someone in the town this morning, someone that she believed had been dead for four years. Just a case of mistaken identity I think, but she seemed very sure.'

'Did she say who this person was?'

'I think she said Sharon something or other. The kids were making such a racket I was only half listening.'

'Well, you have my card if you remember anything else, Mr Pritchard. We are very sorry for your loss.'

'Why did this have to happen to my wife, inspector? She was a good sort, do anything for anybody. She spent hours baking for this fete. There's no justice.'

'Believe me, Mr Pritchard, we will get justice for your wife's murder.'

Chapter 7

The offices of Chase/Colbourne were quiet on a Saturday, operating on a skeleton staff. They had closed early today to enable their employees to attend the fete. Joseph Chase and Andrew Colbourne were sponsors of the event, and encouraged everyone to go along and support it.

Elizabeth Colbourne walked down the corridor to the office she used to share with her husband. She had until last year been a member of the board of directors, but after a prolonged spell of bad health, she had decided to resign, thus spending more time with Andrew, who had already handed over the reins to Mark. At the age of sixty-two, she was still an attractive woman, her blonde hair coiled into a neat French pleat, her make-up perfect. To those who didn't know Elizabeth well, she came over as forbidding and aloof, but there was a softer side to her shown only to the chosen few. She was an astute businesswoman, but her family always came first.

Elizabeth opened the door of her husband's office, surprised to see Chris Chase sitting at Andrew's desk riffling through the drawers.

'Looking for something, Chris?' she asked, an edge to her voice. She was aware of the resentment Chris had displayed after Mark's promotion, and didn't trust him an inch.

'Stapler,' Chris said, slamming the drawer shut, 'Mine's disappeared and I can't seem to find Andrew's either.'

'He keeps it by the photocopier,' she said, picking it up and handing it to him.

He grinned sheepishly, 'Well, I'll get back to my office then.'

'Didn't you go to the fete?' Elizabeth asked, 'Mark and Jo were there.'

'Yes of course I went,' Chris said impatiently. He didn't feel inclined to stand here any longer exchanging pleasantries with her, 'I got out early due to some disturbance in the fortune teller's tent. Anyway, what are you doing here? You don't work here any more.'

'Andrew left a folder, and he wants to check it out over the weekend. I think the heat was too much for him, he came over a bit woozy, so I dropped him off at home.'

'Probably had too much whisky!' said Chris, 'What folder are you looking for?'

'The Winterbourne file. It's in Andrew's safe.'

Chris stood up straight, 'Well, I'll leave you to it.'

He left the room, leaving the door ajar. Elizabeth went across and shut it firmly. She wondered if Chris had also been looking for that file. It had originally been his baby, but after seeing the way things were going, Andrew and Joseph decided to take him off the project.

The Winterbourne project was a contract for a new housing estate with shops and a new community and leisure centre, but Chris was all for it going right through a conservation area. Mark had another site in mind, further away from the town, and proposed to include some starter homes as well as the larger properties that local young people could not afford, thus forcing them away from the place they had grown up in and had always called home.

But Chris knew this would greatly devalue the properties, and he was not above accepting a few backhanders if that was the way to get this off the ground. Mark was a conservationist, building on a green belt was not on his radar.

Chris thumped his fist down hard on the desk, 'Damn Andrew! This had been an ideal opportunity to get hold of that file. He would have found it if Elizabeth hadn't walked in. Chris knew the combination to the safe. Damn! Damn!

Damn!'

Elizabeth tucked the file safely under her arm and walked out of the room, noticing the stapler still on the desk where Chris had dropped it. She would get Andrew to change the code to the safe.

* * * * *

The golf club bar was busy. People had flocked in there after being turfed out of the fete, and the events of the afternoon were all the gossip. Several different stories were flying about, but no one could say for sure what had happened. They only knew that someone had died, and that made for speculative conversation.

Chris carried two glasses of champagne to a table away from the general babble, and handed one to the young woman sitting there.

'So, have you spoken to your uncle about what we talked about?' Kelsey Emmerson asked, taking a sip of the champagne, feeling the bubbles hit her face - not an unpleasant sensation, it reminded her of what she was drinking.

Chris sighed, 'Nothing doing, I'm afraid. The meeting hasn't taken place yet and I don't think Joseph's going to back me up. And now with all this business over the Winterbourne project, well it doesn't exactly put me in a good light. My uncle keeps reminding me we are an ethical company and they're not prepared to bulldoze through that heath, so it's not looking good.'

'I thought you were going to do a bit of revamping on that file. What happened? Did you get cold feet?'

Chris sneered. He hated it when she made him sound wimpish. 'Of course not! I almost got it. Then that interfering old busybody Elizabeth came in. She's got the file now, and short of mugging her for it, there's not a lot I can do!'

'Chris, you have to fight for this. You have as much

right to be on the board of directors as Mark does. Okay, he's got more clout now he's actually on the board, but you can stick a few spanners in the works. My father will see you right, he's been working towards this estate being built for a couple of years, and we can't let a field of daisies and butterflies get in the way!'

She was right, Chris reflected. If this project went ahead it would mean millions for them all. They say behind a powerful man is a more powerful woman, and Kelsey was the strongest woman he'd ever come across.

She had been working as a receptionist for her father's company when they had first met, and had worked her way to the top within three years. A blonde, blue-eyed beauty, Chris had been smitten from the very start, and could hardly believe his luck when she had agreed to go out with him. He was never quite sure whether it was him she wanted, or his uncle's company. She seemed to show a great interest in what was going on at Chase/Colbourne, and Chris couldn't see any harm in providing her with the details, they were engaged, after all. Kelsey would soon be one of the family, if he could only get her to agree to set the date.

'I think we should set the date for the wedding,' he said, watching as she downed her glass and held it out to him to get her another.

'What's the rush?'

'I can't think of any good reason to wait,' he replied.

She leaned across the table and ran the edge of her tongue round her lips. Grabbing his tie to pull him closer, she smiled seductively, 'Get yourself on the board, and I'll marry you by the end of the year!'

Chapter 8

Lee

Monday morning dawned, bright and sunny. Another hot day was forecast, and I was not looking forward to working in my stuffy house when I could be out in the sunshine. I was a translator, fluent in Italian and French, although I had no idea if I'd studied these languages at university. But the work kept arriving on my doorstep so I wasn't complaining!

I made myself some toast and coffee and sat down at the kitchen table to read the newspaper. It was comfortably warm, the sun hadn't reached its blazing height at this time in the morning, although it was streaming in through the window, I watched the dust motes dance around as I took a bite of toast and opened the paper. Nothing much of interest in there today, until I turned the page and saw Eve's face staring out of it at me. I read on, shocked to find that she had been the victim of Saturday's accident at the fete. Transfixed, I read on, then folded the paper and laid it on the table. Eve Pritchard had been a wife, mother and charity worker. A valued member of the community. Why would anyone want to kill her?

So she had been at the fete after all, and working in the tea tent. But of course Flynn and I had gone straight to the beer tent, and it was conceivable that my attention could have been elsewhere when she'd taken that fateful walk to the fortune teller's tent.

My mind went into overdrive. Was her death anything to do with her mistaking me for Shannon earlier that day? Was there something about Shannon that someone wanted to keep hidden? I cast my mind back to Saturday morning, trying to remember if there had been anyone within earshot of our conversation. But of course I drew a blank. I grinned wryly, I should be used to that by now!

I got out my laptop. Googling Eve would be pointless, it would only tell me about her life, when what I needed was for her to tell me about mine! But that was never going to happen now.

I felt that knowing more about myself was key to unravelling this mystery, so I googled 'Lee Filmer, Manchester.' What came up were details of the car accident. The inquest had shown that my parents car had swerved to avoid another car travelling at great speed, half way over their side of the road. Tyre tracks had supported this theory. My father had then lost control of the car and we had spiralled down the embankment, ending in the gateway of a field. My parents had been killed outright, I had been found unconscious in the back seat, by a man called Jason Webb. This was my first lead. I would google him when I came off this web page. The article then went on to say I had been 24 years old at the time, the only child of Simon and Angela Filmer and that I was a graduate in languages. So I had been to university then! But it didn't mention which one. I wondered why I had not checked all this out when I was living in my parents' home before moving here. But the doctor had advised against digging too deeply into my past, it wouldn't serve any useful purpose and might even impede my recovery. If I was going to remember anything it had to come back naturally. The article did not mention any other relatives. The only person who could have answered my questions about that was the aunt who had left me her cottage. And she was dead too!

I studied the photo the paper had printed. It was of a much younger me, my hair was lighter, I was slightly plumper, and wearing something I would not be seen dead in now!

After checking out Jason Webb and finding that he was still living at the same address, I closed down the computer and grabbing my bag, hurried out to the car, the pile of unworked translations still sitting on my desk. They would have to wait!

I headed for the library, where I asked for all the newspapers printed during the week after the crash. It was all automated now, so I sat down, resolved to scrawling through screen after screen until I found what I was looking for. The break came early, on the third page of the first newspaper. A detailed account of the crash, but nothing I didn't already know, and it also confirmed that Jason Webb lived in a village I was familiar with just outside Manchester, giving his full address as no.10 Mill Row. There was a picture of the mangled car, but thankfully not the picture of the younger me I had googled at home. There had been no trace of the other car involved, just its skid marks on the road proving that it had been there, but of course there were no CCTV cameras on a quiet road in the middle of the night. What had happened to that other car? How could they have driven off, leaving three injured people in the wreck of a car crash that they had been responsible for? Had they even stopped to find out or had they just driven off into the night without a care for what had just happened? Human nature never failed to amaze me, often in a good way, but sometimes in a situation like this I wondered if they were human at all! I guess it was all down to self preservation, they didn't want a brush with the law so got themselves away from the situation as quickly as possible! Then I began to wonder where my family had been going, my passport had been in my bag so perhaps they were taking me to the airport, but a lack of luggage seemed to dispel this theory.

I was just about to close the computer down when a name on a neighbouring page caught my eye. Shannon! I honed in on that and what I found made my heart thump violently.

Shannon was the only daughter of Joseph and Isla Chase, 24 years old, and a teacher in languages. She had been found dead on the same day as my accident, believed to have fallen off the balcony of the family home. How's that for coincidence, my inner voice was saying, but it was more than that. Somehow my past was linked with hers, but I had no idea how that could be.

But one thing I did feel sure of, I was now convinced more than ever that the chance meeting I had with Eve was significant in her death.

What I saw next completely took my breath away. Shannon's picture appeared on the screen and it was like looking in a mirror! This was an up-to-date photo, and every feature was correct, right down to the tiny mole above our right eyebrows. I began to hyperventilate - I had to get outside into the fresh air.

I grabbed my bag and ran from the library, this was freaking me out! I was Lee! My accident had been documented in the papers, but so had Shannon's story. She was lying dead under the window in her father's house, I was unconscious in a wrecked car in a field somewhere near Manchester. I couldn't be in two places at once, neither could I be two people!

I reached the car, but was too keyed up to drive. I took a few deep breaths and gradually felt my body relax. I turned the key in the ignition and pulled out of the car park.

As I drew near to my turn-off, I noticed a car racing towards me at breakneck speed, I swerved onto the grass verge as it flew past, was this how it happened with my family on that fateful night?

Nothing stirred in my memory. But suddenly I had the feeling that I was falling, then looking up and seeing the outlines of two people staring down at me. It was so real. I stopped the car on the grass verge and sat trying to process what was happening to me. Was this just another hallucination, or was it a flashback of something I had actually experienced? Or was I slowly going out of my mind? But no, the evidence was there on the library computer. I took my phone out of my bag and called Flynn.

'For heaven's sake calm down, Lee!' Flynn spoke abruptly, 'You weren't hurt and your car isn't damaged. Okay, I know you've had a shock but the best thing you can do is to go home and relax. Have a brandy or something!'

It was obvious he didn't welcome my call and was making light of what had just happened to me. But for me, being run off the road was a big thing, especially after just reading about the other car crash I'd been in! I decided not to mention the flashback that I'd experienced after I had stopped on the grass verge. He wasn't going to be receptive to that! Perhaps I'd caught him at a bad time, he was probably at work and my interruption was inconvenient, but he said he'd be there for me so who else could I call?

'What make of car was it?' he asked.

I thought for a minute, but all I could remember was that it was a red sporty looking thing, 'Sorry, Flynn, I was too busy trying to stay on the road to notice the make. Just that it was red, sporty and coming at me really fast!'

'Sounds like Mark Colbourne' Flynn replied, 'He's the only one I know that has a car that resembles that description, and he's known for his madcap driving. Thinks that just because he has a posh car, that he owns the road and expects everyone else to get out of his way! He'll have an accident one day!'

'He came close to it this morning' I said drily. 'Do you think I should report it? Before he does someone a serious injury?'

'Without the car registration number you've no proof that it was him. He'll only deny it and because of who he is he'll get away with it. And it won't stop him racing around like he's on the Brands Hatch circuit!'

'Did I interrupt anything important?' I asked after a pause, 'You seemed a bit annoyed when I called.'

'It just shook me up a bit when you said you'd had a close call on the road. I've lost people close to me in road traffic accidents. But no, you didn't interrupt anything important.'

I heard shuffling in the background, Flynn wasn't alone. I supposed he was in the office of wherever it was he was working. And did I hear someone whispering? But I had taken up enough of his time, and I was feeling better after speaking to him, so it was time to ring off and leave him in peace.

'Okay, I think I can get home now without freaking out. Mark Colbourne must be miles away by now and the worst I'll come across on these country lanes is a tractor!'

He laughed, 'Highly dangerous! Especially if you want to get somewhere in a hurry!'

I dropped the phone back into my bag and started the engine. Hopefully the rest of the journey would be uneventful!

Chapter 9

Frank Hutton was driving back to the station, his new Sergeant in the passenger seat. Paul Halliday had been drafted in to deputise for Stephanie Lang, who had fallen on Sunday morning and broken her ankle. Stephanie was now relegated to working on the station's paperwork from her home.

Paul Halliday had been stationed at the Dengate HQ, and was keen to work with Hutton, having heard good things about him from colleagues.

They had just come from interviewing Yvonne Whitmore. She had been working in her garden and was not best pleased at the interruption by the officers.

'Miss Whitmore,' Hutton began, after he had introduced Halliday, 'I have one or two more questions I'd like to ask about Saturday afternoon, if you don't mind'

'And if I do?' Yvonne had replied, 'I'm busy, inspector, as you can see. I told you all I know on Saturday.'

'Not quite,' Hutton said meaningfully, 'You told us you went to the tea tent during your break, but I have a witness that says you were not there. Can you explain that?'

'Your witness is mistaken.'

'My witness happens to be my own sergeant, the one who sat with you when you were so distraught after finding the body. So where were you during your break?'

'Are you suggesting I had something to do with it, inspector? I had the shock of my life when I went into that tent and found that woman like that!'

'I'm not accusing you of anything, Miss Whitmore, but there are some discrepancies in your statement that need clearing up. So I ask you again, where were you between

3pm and 3.20, and the truth this time, please.'

Yvonne put down her gardening shears and looked at the detectives, 'I did go to the tea tent, but there was nowhere to sit, so I took my tea outside. I met up with someone I knew from the village and we stood talking until I went back to my tent.'

'Why didn't you tell us that before?' Hutton demanded. 'It would have saved us coming out to question you again. The truth generally leads to people being exonerated from crimes, keeping information back just leads to confusion and suspicion.'

'I'm sorry, inspector. I suppose I hadn't thought it was relevant, I was on a tea break, I got a cup of tea. What does it matter where I drank it?'

Hutton ignored her question, 'This friend, does he or she have a name?'

'Kelsey Emmerson, and she's not a friend. To tell the truth I don't really like her, but she seemed in the mood to chat. I was a bit surprised, she's a bit snobby and normally wouldn't give me the time of day! She's engaged to Chris Chase from Chase/Colbourne Enterprises. I'm not in that social circle, they would consider themselves superior to the likes of me. But she was friendly enough on Saturday afternoon and was with me the whole time I was on my break. Check it with her if you like.'

'We will' Hutton replied, 'We'll leave you to your gardening, goodbye Miss Whitmore.'

* * * * *

Hutton and Halliday stood in the reception area of Emmerson Associates offices. The receptionist had told them to take a seat while she rang through to Kelsey.

They remained standing till the girl on the desk said to go through the swing doors. Kelsey's door was third on the left.

Kelsey stood by the window looking out at the heat-scorched grass, usually so lush and green, now brown, with the soil showing beneath it, cracked and dry.

She turned as the officers knocked and entered the room as she called out, 'Come in.'

Hutton introduced himself and Halliday, who was bowled over by the stunning young woman in front of him.

'Miss Emmerson,' Hutton began, 'We are investigating the murder of Eve Pritchard who was killed Saturday afternoon at the Dengate fete. I'm sure you will have heard all about it?'

Kelsey nodded, 'Yes, I've heard, inspector, but I can't see what this has to do with me. I was just there to support the fete, but of course I'll help in any way I can.'

'What time did you arrive?' Hutton asked.

'Oh, about 2.15, it might have been a little later. I believe it started at 1pm. I thought I'd give it time to get going before I got there.'

'Did you by any chance come into contact with Yvonne Whitmore?'

Kelsey appeared to be thinking, then, 'As a matter of fact I did, she was coming out of the tea tent. We stood talking for a bit, then she went back to the fortune teller's tent. I really think she believes she can tell fortunes, poor deluded fool! Your future is what you make it, inspector, don't you agree?'

'What time was it when you were speaking to Miss Whitmore?' Hutton asked, not wanting to get into the ins and outs of fortune telling, although it would make his job a whole lot easier sometimes if he had prior knowledge of when a crime was about to be committed.

'About 3 o'clock. Why? I didn't realise I was going to need an alibi! I'd have paid more attention to what I was doing!'

'As far as we're aware, Miss Emmerson, you don't need an alibi. We're just acting on information we've been given. I don't suppose you saw anyone hovering around the fortune teller's tent while you were talking to Yvonne

Whitmore?'

'I didn't see anything suspicious if that's what you mean, but then again, inspector, I wasn't particularly looking.'

'Well, thank you for your time, Miss Emmerson,' Hutton said, ready to go before Halliday's eyes popped right out of his head.

Halliday handed her a card. 'You can contact me on that number if you think of anything that might help,' he said.

She looked at him seductively, 'I certainly will, sergeant.' She watched as the detectives went out and shut the door behind them. Then she picked up the phone and punched in a number, 'I've had the police round here. Get them off my back, will you? I've got enough on my plate without them sniffing round!'

Hutton and Halliday walked out of the building and then sat in the car looking back at it. It was a strange, imposing building, several stories high, constructed of yellow bricks and like the Chase/Colbourne building, glass fronted. Impressive on its own but stuck out like a sore thumb among most of the other more traditionally constructed buildings in the industrial area.

'So, what do you think, Halliday?' Hutton asked.

'About the building sir? Or the girl?'

'Lets start with the girl.'

Halliday drew a deep breath, 'Well, she's certainly a looker, sir. But I don't think I'd trust her. Do you think she's telling us all she knows?'

'I think she would manipulate anyone to get what she wants and I don't think she was particularly pleased to see us either.'

'But she did confirm Yvonne Whitmore's alibi.'

'And by that, also confirming her own. Strange isn't it Halliday, how everyone says they'll help in any way they can, and then go out of their way to avoid answering our questions!'

Chapter 10

Lee

I hadn't expected Flynn to understand, why should he? I couldn't get my head round it myself, but I wasn't prepared for quite such negativity about finding out about my past. He was determined to keep me focusing on the future, and if I was honest, I guess that's what I would have advised to someone else in this position. I had to agree, this wasn't doing my stress levels any good!

'Flynn, I really need you to support me. I haven't got anyone else I can turn to. If the boot was on the other foot you'd want to find out about yourself, wouldn't you?' I was appealing to him to understand how important this was to me.

'I suppose so,' he answered, 'But I hope you know what you're getting into. You might not like what you find, and it could be dangerous. You already believe someone doesn't want you around because, ridiculous as it sounds, somehow you've convinced yourself that Eve Pritchard was murdered because she thought she recognised you. Why give them further grounds to harm you?'

I looked at him pleadingly. He smiled and capitulated, 'Okay, let's look at what we know so far. You saw a picture of a girl in the library that looked like you. But that girl is dead. How can digging around in her past help you discover yours?'

'I'm just looking for answers, Flynn. I've got to start somewhere and this seems to be a good place.'

He sighed, 'So this girl, Shannon, is the daughter of Joseph Chase of Chase/Colbourne Enterprises.'

'Did you know her?' I butted in, 'You've lived here a lot longer than I have.'

'I obviously know of the family, everyone does who lives in this area, They provide employment for half the town from what I gather. But I never knew any of them personally. And the firm has only been in Dengate a couple of years. They were originally based in the Manchester area.'

'Manchester! That's where I lived before moving down here. It's where Shannon died, and where I had that accident. Everything points back to Manchester! And now we all seem to have ended up here in Dengate! Doesn't that strike you as odd?'

'Not particularly. It's a well known fact that a lot of big firms moved their head offices down here when the new industrial/financial area sprang up. They came from all over, Manchester, London, even one from Cardiff if I remember rightly. It's a great area, Lee, out in the country but near enough to the city if they need to get there in a hurry.' He appeared to be thinking for a moment, then spoke again with feeling,

'You know that newspaper might have printed the wrong photograph. Maybe they had a more recent one of you, they had two stories of girls of a similar age involved in tragedies on the same day, you have a bit of a resemblance to each other and they just printed the wrong picture with the wrong story.'

'A bit of a resemblance is the understatement of the year, Flynn! We are a mirror image of each other. But I agree, newspapers don't always get it right.'

Flynn had a way of rationalising everything, and the more I thought about it, the more I had to concede that he might be right. After all, Shannon and I had never met, coincidences happen all the time, and maybe someone just doesn't like the look of my face around these parts. But then there was Eve Pritchard. And no matter what Flynn said, I still believed all this had stemmed from her confusing me with Shannon.

'Maybe I should go see Joseph Chase.' I suggested.

'I don't think that's a good idea, Lee. He never got over the death of his daughter, he won't have her name spoken in his presence. Think what that would do to an old man if you turn up on his doorstep, the facsimile of his dead daughter.'

'Sounds like he needs grief counselling,' I observed, 'Okay, I wouldn't want to upset him, but what about Mark? He's not so closely involved, it's not like she was his sister or anything, and it's been four years. He'll have moved on by now. And I can pull him up over his driving!' I added with a grin.

'Lee, please don't drag any of those people into your fantasies, at least until you know there's something tangible to tell them.'

I pulled a folded sheet of A4 paper out of my pocket. 'This is no fantasy. I found it shoved through the door when I got back from the library this morning.'

He unfolded the note and had the grace to look shocked. The note had been printed with an inkjet printer and arrived without an envelope. Flynn read the words out loud. 'Go back where you came from. You do not belong here.'

'Have you had any more of these?' he asked.

'That's the only one. Should I take it to the police?'

'I don't know how seriously they take anonymous letters,' he answered, 'It's not exactly threatening. Could be some crank's idea of a joke.'

'Well, it's not very funny. There's someone out there who doesn't want me around, and I am going to find out why.'

Flynn looked thoughtful, the note seemed to have made an impact on him that all the other stuff I'd told him hadn't. It was the tangible evidence he'd been looking for, right there in his hand.

He broke the silence at last, 'How do you fancy a trip to

Manchester?'

Chapter 11

Christopher Chase was pacing up and down in his office. The board meeting was in progress and they would be voting on his application to become a member of the board.

He was nervous, he knew he wasn't popular in the same way Mark was, but he was determined and got results. If this did not go his way Kelsey would make him pay!

He thought about the Winterbourne project. He still hadn't managed to get his hands on that file, and it was important to him, and Kelsey, that Mark's proposition didn't go ahead. They would lose millions, and he might lose Kelsey!

He looked round the room, as if seeing it for the first time. It had been his father's office once, until Ezra had unexpectedly died from a heart attack less than a year ago. The tall bookcase holding Ezra's books stood in the corner, books on business and finance mostly. Chris took one from the shelf and leafed through it. His concentration was just not there this afternoon, and he thrust the book back between two others on the shelf.

He glanced down at the passers by from his window. He was sweating hard, so he opened the window a little way to let the cooler air from outside wash over him. Not that it was a lot cooler, but the temperature had dropped a few degrees from the oppressive heat of yesterday.

The door opened and Joseph Chase stood in the doorway. Chris turned abruptly, 'Well?'

Joseph shook his head, 'I'm sorry, the board don't feel you're ready yet. Maybe next year………'

'So you didn't come through for me. Thanks a bunch,

uncle! I suppose Mark contested it and everyone went along with him. Well I'm not so gullible, I don't need this firm, and I don't need you.'

He slammed out of the door, leaving Joseph stunned by his outburst. He'd always known his nephew to have a volatile nature, but this was the first time he'd experienced it first-hand.

* * * * *

Chris drove madly along the road, slowing down when he neared his uncle's home. This house had once been his home and if he was honest he missed living there. He'd had his own apartment which was almost as large as the apartment he now occupied, a luxury modern apartment with all the latest gadgets, some of them just status symbols; Chris would never use half of them. And he missed the busy comings and goings that were always present in his uncle's house. The place seemed alive; now he sat alone most of the time in luxury and a mocking silence. Did the luxurious surroundings make up for the loss of the company of the people he'd been close to? Kelsey would say yes, definitely. She was a material girl and used to living well and getting everything she wanted, she didn't seem to need people and thought Chris shouldn't either! His relationship with his uncle had not been the same since he'd moved out, Joseph had not understood that now he was engaged, Kelsey had to come first with him. And Chris had been right, hadn't he? His uncle had let him down, so where was his family loyalty?

The house would be empty right now, everyone was at the office, including Elizabeth, and that had rankled as she was no longer a member of the board herself.

The Winterbourne project paperwork was in that house somewhere. It had to be. It wasn't in the office, Chris had searched. He made up his mind all of a sudden, and turned the car into the lane that lead up the hill to his Uncle's property.

He stopped the car in front of the Georgian-style building. It was impressive, with its white painted windows comprised of individual small squares and the columns either side of the main entrance. A white front door completed the effect.

Chris took out his keys and unlocked the front door, his uncle had probably forgotten he still had them, but it saved him the trouble of breaking in! On entering the house he experienced a sudden feeling of melancholy as he looked round the vast hallway with its pale green painted walls, brilliant white doors and a magnificent staircase leading to the upper floor. Not for the first time, he wished Kelsey had allowed him to stay on there. But she was determined he should buy one of the new penthouse suites that had sprung up a few years ago. It overlooked the river and Chris couldn't deny he was very comfortable there, but it wasn't and never would be where he felt he belonged. He glanced briefly at a framed photograph on the wall, of his Aunt Isla sitting on a sea wall somewhere in Cyprus. Chris had been close to his aunt, who had been a great comfort to him after the death of his father.

But now he was on his own, apart from Kelsey who appeared to be fighting his corner, but although Chris was loath to admit it, Kelsey had an agenda of her own.

He made straight for Joseph's study. That was the most likely place to begin searching. His eyes went straight to the picture on the wall, a country scene by John Constable, behind which was the safe. This one Chris did not have the combination to, so if the file was in there he was snookered.

He began with the desk drawers. The top drawer contained mostly stationary equipment and papers. There was nothing of interest in the second one either, just a lot of old photos, mostly sepia in colour, of long dead members of Joseph's family. He thumbed through them thinking what a stern lot they looked. Did no one smile for photographs in those days?

His eyes rested on a more up-to-date one of a young girl, the young girl he had seen around town. She was standing with her back against a tree, and she wore a blue and white polka dot dress. She was smiling into the camera, her long hair tucked behind her ears, her eyes shining. She looked so alive, so pretty. He hadn't appreciated his cousin when she was alive, he'd never really looked at her properly. And now it appeared she was back and living somewhere in the Dengate area. He'd seen her himself around town once or twice, he'd stared at her but she had just looked away. But this kind of thinking was nuts! It couldn't be Shannon. Shannon was dead, he'd found her body himself. And he didn't believe in ghosts!

He opened the last drawer and drew out an envelope addressed to Joseph in bold handwriting. It was yellowed with age, as was the folded paper he extracted from it. He unfolded it and began to read, realising as soon as he started that this was important. This could prove very useful to him, even more so than the Winterbourne file. Coming to the end of the text, he wondered what would have happened if this had come to light during his father's day. It would have altered the whole concept of the partnership between the Chases and the Colbournes. Kelsey was going to love this!

He pocketed the letter, and then folded a piece of plain paper and slipped it into the envelope, carefully placing it back in the drawer exactly as he had found it.

He left the house with a smile on his face, he held the trump card now, and he was not afraid to use it!

Chapter 12

Lee

The Star Inn was large establishment just outside the city, and lay well back from a busy road. It had a restaurant, although Flynn and I arrived far too late to make use of it. We had stopped at a motorway café for a coffee and a sandwich, but now the hunger pangs were kicking in again.

'Did you book one or two rooms?' Flynn asked casually, as we drove along. The sun was low in the sky, almost blinding from the side window. I twisted the visor round to stop the glare.

'Two,' I answered, 'You know how I feel about getting into a relationship while my head's all over the place. That's why it's so important for me to find myself. I can't concentrate on anything but that at the moment. I can't move on till I know exactly who I am – in more ways than one!'

'It's okay,' he answered, and I immediately felt guilty. To me Flynn was just a friend, a good friend who had put up with all my insecurities and I know his negativity was all about keeping me safe. If he was looking for something more than friendship, I was going to be a big disappointment to him. Maybe one day, when this was over…. But I didn't want to think about that at the moment.

The rooms were sparsely furnished, but clean and comfortable. We had en suite bathrooms and free Wi-Fi.

We just had time for a quick drink in the bar before closing time and we sat in the lounge with long cool beers and crisps. That would have to do till breakfast time!

'I think we should start with Jason Webb,' I told him, 'At least we know where he lives. Then I need to find out more about my aunt. I feel bad moving into her house and I don't even know what she looks like!'

'So where do we start looking for her? She's dead too, or you wouldn't be living in her house.'

'The solicitor's letter said she had been living in a care home for the last two years. If we could find that there might be someone who remembers her. She appears to have had some form of dementia, so she must have written her will before she got sick. There doesn't seem to have been anyone acting as power of attorney.'

'Okay, it's your call. Jason first though. At least we've got someone who's still alive!'

* * * * *

The next morning dawned bright and sunny. Flynn wanted a leisurely breakfast, but I wanted to get going as soon as possible. Who knew where this paper-chase would lead? We were out on the road again before nine o'clock, and heading towards Mill Row. I seemed to know instinctively which direction to go in, though I couldn't remember anything about the area. We parked in a lay-by just outside the village, deciding to walk the rest of the way. It was a beautiful morning, not too hot so far. I was glad of the pashmina I'd thrown over my shoulders, as the temperature here was several degrees cooler than down south.

Jason's house was one of a pair of semi-detached properties at the top end of the cul-de-sac. The front garden was typical of houses built in this style, with a concrete path bordered by grass, and a circular flower bed in the middle of it containing a single rose bush. Nice, but very suburban.

Jason himself was a heavily built man, slightly balding, with trousers hanging over what amounted to a beer belly. He wore a T-shirt with the motif of a rock band on the front.

'Mr Webb,' I began, 'I'm Lee Filmer. You may not remember me, but you saved my life when I was involved in a car accident four years back.'

He stared at me for a few seconds, then spoke, 'Ah yes. Lee Filmer. I heard you moved away.'

'I did. The thing is I lost all memory of the accident and everything that happened before it, so I'm trying to piece bits together and wondered if you would be able to help me?'

'You better come in,' he said, showing us into a sitting room where an equally large woman sat with her feet up on a footstool. The TV was blaring and she picked up the remote control and muted it.

'Betty, my wife,' Jason said, and then to Betty, 'This is the lass I found in that car smash I told you about.'

'Hello, Mrs Webb. Sorry to intrude. This is my friend Flynn Wyatt.'

'Sit down,' she said, swinging her legs to the floor, 'Jason's told me all about that night. You had a lucky escape.'

'I'm very grateful to your husband for what he did,' I continued, 'I would have come before to thank him, but I lost my memory in the crash, and I still don't really know what happened. I'm hoping Jason can fill in the gaps.'

Jason sat down in a king-sized armchair, 'I don't know what I can tell you, lass. I was coming home late that night after a trip to Scotland, and was almost home when I saw the car on its side in a gateway to a field. I didn't know how long ago it had happened but thought I'd better take a look. The people in the front seat were beyond help, and you were unconscious in the back seat. I thought I could smell a whiff of petrol so I had to get you out in case it blew. Then I called an ambulance and the police turned up shortly after that. That's all I can tell you.'

'And you are absolutely certain it was me you pulled

out of that car?'

'Well, who else would it be? I wouldn't claim to know your family, but I'd seen you around the village enough times to recognise you.' After my release from hospital I had stayed at my parents' home, but had not ventured far from the village. Nothing about the family home was familiar. I hadn't recognised them from their photos and found nothing amongst their papers to give me a hint of my past life as their daughter. But I did come across certain papers relating to me, my old school reports, my parents had kept them right from primary school. I had been far from a model student, apparently, but had improved over the years and had left school with reasonably good grades. I didn't remember anything about my school days, it was like reading about a stranger! And there were photos right from when I was first born, all through my school years and a few holiday snaps taken in various parts of the world. I'd had all those experiences, yet they were now totally lost to me.

'Mr Webb,' I tried a different angle, 'Did you know my aunt, Millicent Palmer? She spent the last few years of her life in a care home, Sunnyside House?'

Jason shook his head, but Betty sat up from her slouched position, 'I knew Millie. Lovely lady. I was sorry to hear she'd died.'

'Do you know if she was happy at Sunnyside?'

Betty pulled a face, 'Seemed to be. But she went a bit funny in the head towards the end. Wasn't always living in the real world. Came out with a lot of funny old stuff sometimes. No one ever knew if anything she said was true or not!'

'How did you know her, Mrs Webb?' asked Flynn.

'My father was in there for a while. Millie used to play cards with him.' She got up and opened a drawer in the bureau. She handed me a photograph. 'That was taken two Christmases ago, they had a bit of a shindig at the home. That's your aunt with my father. You can keep it if you like, I can get another one done.'

'That's very kind, Thank you,' I stood up to go. 'Thank you both for your time…. How far is Sunnyside from here?' I asked as an afterthought.

'Turn right at the junction. It's about a ten-minute drive.'

Chapter 13

Lee

Jason's estimation of a ten-minute drive turned out to be nearer twenty. We found the care home at the end of a short turning, a large red brick building with a huge conservatory on the side.

The sun was high in the sky now, and I left the pashmina in the car, these places were too hot at the best of times, without the sun adding to it.

Inside, I was pleasantly surprised, a large free-standing fan was blowing cool air around the reception area. The woman on the desk smiled as we approached. 'Good Morning. Can I help you?'

'My aunt, Millicent Palmer lived here until her death in February. I was wondering if there was anyone who knew her and could talk to me about her?'

Her smile vanished, 'I'm sure there was nothing untoward about her death. She had dementia, it followed the normal course. Your aunt died of natural causes.'

'We weren't suggesting otherwise,' Flynn said, 'Miss Filmer was involved in an accident four years ago and has no memory of that day, or any time before it. She doesn't remember her aunt, and wants to get to know her through other people who do remember her.'

I wondered how many more times we were going to have to repeat that, it was beginning to sound like a record stuck in a groove!

The receptionist relaxed, 'I see. Well, I didn't know the residents personally, but Vicky might be able to help you. She's been here the longest.'

She paged Vicky, and a few minutes later a middle-aged woman in a pale blue overall and with an air of authority came out.

'You wanted to see me?' she said briskly.

We launched into the story once again, and then Vicky took us into a pleasant room with soft grey painted walls and pictures of rural scenes hanging on them. A vase of flowers stood in the window sill.

'Pretty room,' I said, looking round.

'Thank you,' she answered, 'We wanted somewhere tranquil for visitors to sit. Sometimes it can be upsetting if their loved one is not having a good day. Anyway, what do you want to know about Millie Palmer?'

'Did she talk about me?' I blundered in, something about this woman was making me edgy. After all Millie had been dead for six months, and Vicky's priorities lay with her current residents. It was clear she didn't want me dragging her back to the past when she was so busy.

'Yes, she spoke of you often. She talked about you as a small child, but she was disappointed you never came to see her. Your mother came regularly, but after the accident, there was no one.'

That answered my next question. I wondered why I felt so upset that I hadn't visited her now, I obviously hadn't worried about it back then! But it explained Vicky's coolness towards me.

'I lost my memory in the accident,' I defended myself, 'I wasn't aware I even had an aunt until I got the solicitor's letter saying she had left me her cottage.'

Vicky straightened her gait, 'Well, that's all in the past. Now if there's nothing else?'

'Please, just tell me about her. Was she happy here? What things did she like doing? I really want to know more about her. I don't remember anything!'

'She was a popular member of our home, Miss Filmer. Liked and respected by staff and residents alike. But of course once the dementia really set in, Millie changed. She became fixated on odd memories from her past, at least we thought they were memories, but as the illness progressed, it became evident she was just rambling, as so many people with the condition do.'

'Was there anything in particular she was concerned about?' I asked.

'Yes, she was very agitated about a child. Kept saying what a shame it was about the baby. But like I said, it was probably the dementia talking.'

'Vicky, I don't suppose you know where I was born?' I asked.

'How on earth would I know that?' she looked daggers at me, we had taken up enough of her time. And the chances of her knowing that were very remote, but suddenly it seemed important to me to find out. Vicky looked at me as if I'd just landed from Mars, or had escaped from the local loony bin, but she could see I really wanted to know, and for the right reasons, so she must have realised how important this was to me.

She softened her gaze, 'I suppose you could try the Helen Rosewell Maternity Home. But I don't know how long their records go back. Now you really must excuse me.'

We thanked her for her time and she shepherded us out of the door.

'Time's getting on,' Flynn informed me, 'How about a spot of lunch?'

It was nearly 2pm so we headed into the city and found a coffee shop that produced an amazing lasagne. I hadn't realised how hungry I was.

'This is as good as my mum used to make,' Flynn declared. He hadn't mentioned his family before, only to say his parents were both dead.

'Tell me about them,' I said.

'They were both doctors. I think they were a bit disappointed when I decided not to follow in their footsteps, but they forgave me,' he said with a grin.

'You must miss them,' I continued.

'Of course, but they say time heals and it does. It's a long time ago now.'

'Well, at least you've got memories of them,' I said, suddenly not wanting to eat any more.

Flynn reached out and touched my hand across the table, 'Memories can get distorted over time. Don't dwell on it. You might not like what you find.'

That didn't seem to matter. Everyone had good and bad memories, but at least they had something. I decided not to press the issue; Flynn was never going to see things my way.

It was nearly 4pm when we left the coffee shop. Too late to pay an unexpected call on the maternity home. 'That's one for tomorrow,' I told Flynn as we got back into the car.

'Lee, I've been thinking. We don't seem to be getting very far with this search. I thought this was going to be just the one night away. I have to get back for work. I think we should go home tonight.'

'Well I don't!' I rounded on him, 'We've only just got started. We can't give up now!'

'Look, why don't you stay here a few days, I'll get the train back and you can use the car. I really need to get back tonight.'

I had to concede; he had a job to go to. So did I, but I'd work all night if necessary to catch up when I got home.

We had got about half way back to the hotel when I looked up and saw a large house at the top of a hill. We had just come through a small village and although that didn't seem familiar to me, this house did. It was a large building with no close neighbours. Had I ever been there? I had to take a closer look.

'What's that place?' I asked Flynn, I seemed to be drawn towards it.

'Just some old house,' he answered, 'Why?'

'I want to take a closer look. Do you think that's where I used to live?'

'Lee, you've got to stop this. It's just a random house, nothing to do with you. And you know where your parents home was. For heaven's sake, you lived there yourself for a few months before you moved to Dengate. It was a much smaller house in the middle of a housing estate! I think this house is way out of your league.'

'We could have lived there once. Maybe we hit hard times and had to sell up and take the rented house' I was clutching at straws, it was beginning to sound crazy even to me, but there was something about this place that I couldn't let go – at least not before checking it out thoroughly. I turned to look at Flynn, 'Take me up there, please. There's something about that house, I don't know what it is, but it seems to be calling me. Does that sound ridiculous?'

'Totally,' he sounded really hacked off, but he turned into the first road that led us up the hill. I watched the house grow bigger as we got nearer.

The house was reminiscent of the 1920s, very symmetrical, creamy white walls, with a flat roof, and the horizontal oblong windows that were typical of that era. I got out of the car and took a few steps forward. Flynn stayed in the car, he had indulged me enough.

I looked up and that was when I saw the balcony. A wrought iron affair, painted black. I took a step backwards and stared up at it. That was when it happened. Once again I had the feeling that I was falling. I heard a rushing sound in my ears, and again I thought I saw two people standing on the balcony, peering down, I was reliving the flashback I'd had when I had looked at that other house in Dengate. Falling, falling, until I hit the ground with a thud. The last thing I heard was the sound of someone screaming. Flynn later told me it was me!

Chapter 14

Lee

Flynn left after an early dinner that evening. I took him to the station and then returned to the hotel. There were all kinds of theories running through my head, the most hopeful being that my aunt had been talking about a real baby. I hoped it was true. If Shannon and I were sisters it would explain the likeness between us in those library photographs. But if there was a child, it could equally have been a boy. That would blow my theory right out of the water! I hoped the maternity home would be able to provide some answers. There was a strong possibility that their records would no longer exist, it had been twenty-eight years after all. And if I had not been born in there they wouldn't be able to help me anyway.

The next morning it was raining, not heavily, but enough to make me wish I'd brought a coat when I'd left Kent. The pashmina was no protection against the rain so I hadn't bothered to bring it with me this morning. Flynn had text earlier to say he got home safely, which was a relief as I'd heard on the news there had been an incident on the railway line, not to mention the inevitable usual delays! I understood why he had to get back, but that didn't stop me wishing I didn't have to do this alone. If the records no longer existed I might as well go home too!

I reached the maternity home just after nine in the morning. The rain had eased to a drizzle as I got out of the car and walked up the steps into the wide foyer. It was nicely decorated in coral pink and lilac. A vast white and chrome desk stood before me, behind which sat a young woman with ginger hair piled up on top of her head.

'Yes, we do still have records,' I was told on approaching the desk and going through the saga of how I was searching for my past once more. 'But of course the older ones are not computerised. You'll have to wade through reams of paper and you might find that you weren't born here after all.'

'I'll take the risk,' I had said. Nothing was going to stop me getting my hands on those records now I'd come this far.

'There might be someone who could help you,' the receptionist was saying, 'Sally Tate has been here since the year dot! She might even remember you being born!'

It was a bit of a long shot, but I was anxious to meet Sally, who turned out to be nearing retiring age and by some miracle did remember my birth.

'Yes, I remember your mother well,' she said, 'That was the surprise of the century! She came in to have her baby and then gave birth to twins!'

This was exactly what I wanted to hear, my heart was thumping hard, and I pressed on extracting information out of this pleasant lady.

'And the babies were both girls?' I asked with my heart in my mouth. I had no objection to having a brother, but I desperately needed this twin to be a girl.

'Yes,' she answered, a look of nostalgia on her face, 'Two beautiful little girls, alike as two peas in a pod.'

'They were identical?'

'Oh yes, except one twin was a bit smaller than the other. The smaller one suddenly got sick and unfortunately didn't survive. Very sad it was.'

My world came crashing down. Shannon had been very much alive until four years ago. Another dead end! There were too many people turning up dead in this case. My parents, Aunt Millicent, my twin sister, Shannon, and of course Eve Pritchard.

Flynn was right. I was never going to find the truth in

Manchester, time to go home. I thanked Sally for her time and went back to the hotel to pack and check out of my room. Slinging my bags in the back seat of the car, I started the engine and pulled out of the car park. As I drove I churned over in my mind all that I had learned. The most important being that I had not been an only child. I had met people who had positively identified me as Lee Filmer, but that didn't explain the photo likenesses in those library pictures. If my twin had lived she could easily have been Shannon, but my sister had not lived past her first week; and Shannon had been 24 when she died. But it did explain one thing – my aunt had not been rambling when she had talked about a baby. My twin sister was the child she had been referring to. If only she had lived! I would have loved to have got to know her, but sadly that was not to be. Would Shannon and I have liked the same things? Had the same taste in fashion? I couldn't see me dressing identically to anyone else though. We were identical twins, but I felt I was very much an individual. Maybe that came from being separated from my sister all these years, until today I had not even known she had existed!

I had not asked Sally where my sister was buried. I could at least take some flowers to her grave before I embarked on the long drive home. I turned back at the first junction and headed straight for the maternity home, just in time to catch Sally before she went off her shift.

She was surprised to see me and suggested a walk round the gardens. 'They're at their best at this time of the year,' she said, glancing at the brightly coloured flower beds, and the variegated leaves of the hostas. 'But you haven't come to talk about gardens, have you?'

I shook my head, 'The receptionist said you'd been here a long time, so you'd have a good idea of what went on back then. I feel there's something you aren't telling me.'

'You're very perceptive. Yes, this place has a history,

but no good can come of bringing it all up again now.'

'It's important, Sally. It might have a bearing on what's happening to me today,' I pleaded with her.

'I doubt that, but I suppose it won't do any harm. The Helen Rosewell Maternity Home was closed down during the year you were born, due to a scandal involving one of our doctors. I can't remember his name, but he died years ago in a road accident, just as your parents did. No one was ever sure exactly what his crime was, it was all kept very hush-hush, but it was enough to close the home down altogether. Of course there were rumours flying around at the time but ....well, it was all a long time ago. Anyway, I took a private nursing job until it opened again eighteen months later under new management, and I was offered my old job back. Now you know as much as I do.'

I was silent for a minute, taking all this in. 'Do you know where my sister is buried?' I asked.

'Your mother was traumatised after the birth. It had been a difficult birth, she lost a lot of blood, which made her very weak. Added to this she now had two babies to care for when she had only been expecting one. Then the baby she had never seen suddenly died. It was not the same back then, where today's mothers are encouraged to stay with their sick child as much as possible. Back then only the nursing staff were allowed in the intensive care unit. The doctor felt it would be better for your mother to focus on the healthy child she had. I don't know what happened to your sister's body. There was probably a private service in the hospital chapel, followed by cremation. I'm sorry you had to hear all that, it must be distressing, but you did ask.'

'I appreciate your honesty. I needed to hear the truth, and in a strange way, you've given me hope,' I replied. After hesitating for a moment I asked, 'What was the cause of my sister's death?'

'I'm not sure, but I think it was breathing difficulties. She was a very sick baby.'

'Did you nurse her while she was ill?'

'No. The doctor appointed another nurse to tend to her. Someone he brought in from an agency. He couldn't spare his regular nurses to give all their attention to one child when there were so many more mothers and babies needing our attention.'

'Was this normal? The practice of bringing in outside staff to look after the ones who were sick?'

'Yes, we thought it a bit strange, but we were always short staffed and it was always the same nurse.'

There was nothing more Sally could tell me.

I said my goodbyes, after giving her a donation towards the new equipment the home was canvassing for, and once more started on the road for home, but this time with hope, not despair.

There was no proof that the child had actually died. Sally and her contemporaries only had this doctor's word for it, and there was no grave. And bringing in an agency nurse seemed to me to be an odd practice. So if the child had survived, Shannon could still have been my twin. I felt an affinity with the Chase/Colbourne family, although I had never actually met any of them. So based on the information Sally had given me, if my sister had somehow defied all odds and lived, where had she spent her childhood? Somehow I had to find out if Shannon had been adopted.

I finally opened my front door a little after 6pm, and dumping my bags in the hallway, picked up the mail from the hall floor.

There was a bill from my solicitor for the work he'd done on the transference of Aunt Millie's cottage to me, and another folded sheet of paper. As before, there was no envelope, and I unfolded it to see the same typeface as before, block capitals and the message was brief, but to the point – and this time it was threatening:

'IF YOU VALUE YOUR LIFE, GO HOME!'

Chapter 15

Christopher Chase marched into his uncle's sitting room where Joseph was having drinks with Andrew and Elizabeth. The French doors were open, letting in the cooler evening air, the fragrance from the roses wafting in through them. Isla had been a keen gardener, the roses were her speciality, and when Joseph sat in the rose garden in the evenings it was almost as if she was with him.

Joseph was now sitting in a wide winged leather armchair, Andrew and Elizabeth on the sofa. The room was furnished with period pieces, and antique artefacts stood on every available surface. The pictures on the wall were either the best copies Christopher had ever seen, or they were the real thing.

Joseph looked up as Christopher entered the room, 'Ah, Chris. Come and join us. Help yourself to a drink.' He nodded towards the drinks cabinet and turned back to Andrew.

Chris poured himself a large whisky and sat down on the other sofa.

'So, what brings you here tonight?' Joseph asked. He had not forgotten Chris's outburst after the last board meeting, and was surprised that his nephew had called on him.

Chris had been annoyed to find Andrew and Elizabeth there, the letter he had found was burning a hole in his pocket, but there would be no chance to confront his uncle with it tonight!

'Just wanted a word with Mark,' Chris said thinking quickly, 'I thought he might be here.'

'We're waiting for Mark and Jo,' said Elizabeth,

'They're obviously running late.'

'What did you want to see Mark for?' asked Joseph. He was wary of Chris's actions now, and felt that he might not have the company's best interest at heart.

'Oh, nothing important. It can wait.' Chris took a swig of his drink, 'Good drop of whisky, uncle,' he said, trying to get the conversation away from the reason why he'd suddenly turned up without warning.

The phone rang and Elizabeth got up to answer it. 'That was Jo. Mark's not home yet, she hasn't heard from him and she's spitting feathers! She's on her way here now. Mark will have to join us later, if he can be bothered!'

She had hardly sat down again when the doorbell rang. She jumped up quickly, 'I'll go.'

'Well that can't be Mark. He'd have come straight in,' said Andrew.

'Yes, I think I've been a bit liberal with the keys to this place. Everyone seems to come and go as they please,' Joseph chuckled.

Elizabeth came back, followed by Hutton and Halliday. 'These gentlemen are from the police,' she said soberly.

Hutton stepped forward, 'I am Detective Chief Inspector Hutton from Barling CID. This is Sergeant Halliday. Which of you gentlemen is Andrew Colbourne?'

Andrew turned towards him, 'I am. What can I do for you, inspector?'

'You might like to talk in private, sir,' Hutton said.

Andrew indicated Elizabeth, 'This is my wife, and these are my friends. You can speak in front of them, inspector.'

'I'm afraid it's bad news, sir,' Hutton began, 'There has been an accident involving your son, Mark. His car ran off the road at Barling Halt. I'm sorry to tell you he didn't survive the accident.'

Elizabeth let out a shriek, the others sat nonplussed. Andrew was the first to speak, 'How and when did this happen?'

'Late this afternoon. It appears he was going at speed, lost control of the car, and ran it off the road. There was no other vehicle involved.'

'That damn car! I told him not to race it around here, but he said it was built for speed.'

'Do you have any idea where Mark was going?' Hutton asked.

'Here. He was on his way here. We thought he was just running late.'

'Do you know if Mark had any enemies, sir?'

'Enemies? No, of course not. Mark was respected by everyone in the company.'

Joseph glanced at his nephew. 'Not by everyone,' he thought silently.

'Why do you ask that, inspector?' asked Andrew, 'Was there something odd about his accident?'

'I'm afraid so, sir. The brake cables had been cut. Somebody intended this to happen.'

'Oh, God, no!' Elizabeth wailed, 'Why would anyone do that?'

'That's what we're going to find out,' Hutton said, pausing to give them a chance to take it all in.

'Mark was married, wasn't he? Do you know the whereabouts of his wife?' he asked.

'She's on her way here. We had a family soirée planned. She rang to say she wasn't going to wait for Mark any longer.'

'Do you mind if we wait?' Hutton said, 'I'd like to talk to her.'

Chris was gripping his glass so tightly he was afraid it might break. So Mark and Jo had been invited to this little soirée, but he had not. Well, things were about to change. With Mark now dead, and also Shannon, that made him the only family member of the original pioneers left. And with the letter safely stowed in his pocket, surely the chairmanship of Chase/Colbourne was in the bag?

Joanna Colbourne arrived with a flourish, bursting into the sitting room all apologies, 'I'm so sorry everyone, I don't know what's keeping Mark. He promised he'd get home on time tonight........Oh' She stopped abruptly on seeing the two police officers in the room.

'Sit down, Jo' said Andrew, 'I'm afraid we have some bad news.'

Joanna sat, now anxious as she looked at her father-in-law, 'What's happened? Is it Mark?'

'I'm sorry, Mrs Colbourne,' Hutton began, 'Your husband died in an accident this afternoon.'

Joanna sat very still, her face had lost all its colour. Then she let out a wail, slowly building till she was almost screaming. Elizabeth put an arm round her, 'Inspector, she's not in any fit state to be questioned. Can't you come back tomorrow?'

'Of course,' Hutton said, starting to get up.

'No. I'm okay. I want to know what happened.' Joanna pulled away from Elizabeth, dabbing at her eyes with a handkerchief.

'If you're sure' Hutton said sitting back down again. He took a deep breath, this was the worst part of his job, seeing the anguish on people's faces as he told them how their loved ones had died.

'It was a car accident,' he began, 'It appears Mark ran off the road when the car went out of control. The brake cables had been cut. Do you have any idea at all who could have done this?'

Joanna looked straight at Christopher, 'Ask him!' she said, a harsh tone to her voice, 'He's been jealous of Mark since they were kids! And when Mark got his promotion it got worse. If anyone had a motive for killing Mark it was Christopher Chase!'

'Mr Chase?' Hutton looked enquiringly at the young man draining the last of the whisky from his glass.

'She's talking rubbish, inspector. It's the shock. Yes, I did feel that promotion should have been mine, but murder!'

'Can you tell us your whereabouts this afternoon?' Hutton asked.

'Well, I certainly wasn't cutting the brake cables on that bloody car! I was at home. I'm taking a break from work so I went to see Kelsey in her office and then spent the rest of the day watching the cricket on TV. You can check with Kelsey if you like.'

'We will, sir. And there's no one who could confirm your whereabouts when you left her?'

'No. I was home alone.'

'What was the purpose of your visit to Kelsey Emmerson, sir?'

'She's my girlfriend! Do I need an excuse to visit her?'

Hutton stood up, Lang followed him, 'I think that's all for now,' he said, 'We will keep you up to date on future developments and if you think of anything we should know about please contact us immediately.'

'You will find out who did this?' said Joanna, 'Someone has to pay for this!'

'We'll do everything we can to see whoever did this is brought to justice, Mrs Colbourne. We're sorry for your loss.'

The family watched in silence as the two police officers left the room. All eyes were on Christopher.

'Oh, you don't seriously think………?' he began, slamming his whisky glass down on the coffee table.

He looked round the room at the hostile stares, shook his head in disbelief and walked out.

Chapter 16

Lee

I walked into the police station at precisely 9am the following morning. I was shown into a room with a large desk and three chairs, one on one side of it, and two on the other. I sat down on one of the pair, the police officer took the one opposite. He was about my age, with dark spiky hair and black rimmed glasses.

'I'm Detective Sergeant Paul Halliday,' he said, 'Shall we start with your name?'

'Lee Filmer,' I told him, 'I don't really know where to start. So much has been happening since I moved to Dengate.'

'And when was that?' he asked.

'About a month ago. My aunt left me her cottage, *Hazeldene* near Barling Halt.' I took a deep breath and continued, 'On the morning of the fete, I was accosted by a woman in the high street, the woman who was killed at the fete later that day. She had mistaken me for someone called Shannon, who I later found out was the daughter of Joseph Chase. Shannon died four years ago, the same day as I was involved in a car accident which wiped out my memory. I can't remember the accident or anything before it.'

I paused, my throat was dry. 'Could I have some water, please?' I asked.

'Of course.' He stood up and left the room, coming back a few minutes later with a glass which he handed to me. I sipped it steadily, then swallowing hard, I continued, telling him about my trip to the library, the visit to Manchester, the care home and the maternity home, and lastly I gave him the anonymous letters.

'Do you have any more of these?' he asked.

I shook my head, 'Just those two. The last one was waiting for me when I got back from Manchester last night.'

'Does anyone else know about these?' He folded the letters up and put them to one side on his desk.

'Just Flynn. Flynn Wyatt. He's a friend who accompanied me to Manchester. I haven't spoken to him since I got home, so he only knows about the first one.'

I hadn't felt inclined to contact Flynn since I'd arrived home. He wasn't taking me seriously and I didn't want to bombard him with any more of my 'fantasies.'

'I was thinking of going to see the Chases,' I told the Sergeant, 'Flynn didn't think that was a good idea. He said it would upset Joseph Chase as I looked so much like Shannon.'

The sergeant smiled kindly, 'I would agree with him for the moment. Let us look into this first. I'll keep you posted every step of the way. In the meantime, Miss Filmer, be careful. If someone wants you out of the way I'd advise you to keep a low profile for the time being.'

That made sense. I felt I could trust this man in a way, I'd come to realise, that I'd never really trusted Flynn, but this guy believed me. Flynn thought I was spinning fantasies, but even he had shown concern over the first anonymous note.

I came away from the police station feeling relieved. I had someone on my side at last. If he was to help me I had to do as he suggested and keep a low profile. So leaving the sleuthing in his capable hands, I decided to do some decorating. My aunt had used the cottage as a holiday home, spending most of the summers in Dengate, the rest of the year in Manchester. But since she had spent her last few years in the care home, the place was in need of complete redecoration. There was a hardware store just down the road so I made straight for that where

I bought paint, brushes and white spirit. The assistant was an elderly man, who looked faintly green when I walked in.

I felt I had to reassure him, 'It's okay, you haven't seen a ghost. It appears I'm Shannon Chase's double. My name is Lee Filmer and I've just moved into Hazeldene Cottage.'

He visibly relaxed, ' Sorry miss, didn't want to appear rude, but you and Shannon are just like two peas in a pod.'

Where had I heard that before?

'That family seems cursed,' he went on, 'First Shannon, and now Mark.'

'Mark Colbourne? Has something happened to him?'

'He was killed in a car accident last night. And rumour has it that it wasn't an accident! The brake cables had been cut.'

'So it was murder.' I could hardly believe what I was hearing. No wonder Sergeant Halliday didn't want me going up there stirring things up. Although no blood relation to Joseph Chase, Mark had been thought of as a son through his long association with the family. He was the natural inheritor of the company, so who would it go to now? Was this some industrial crime? But where did Eve Pritchard fit in?

I gathered up my purchases and went home, my mind on the crash that had killed Mark. Flynn had predicted Mark would have an accident in that car, but he had certainly not known that someone would help him along! This was too much to take in, first Eve, then Mark - and everything had been all right till I came along – the dead spit of Shannon. I wished I'd never heard of Dengate, but I was here now and the council house my parents had rented had been re-let to someone else, so there was no going back. The cottage was my home now and I had to make the best of it!

The first thing I had done when I moved into the

cottage was to give it a thorough cleaning. Armed with brushes and cloths, I had swept, polished and scrubbed for the first few days. I had taken down the curtains and washed them, cleaned out the kitchen cupboards, and washed all the crockery. Later I would get my own furniture out of storage, it was so much more modern and lighter than my aunt's heavy oak sideboards and wardrobes. And I would eventually have the kitchen and bathroom replaced, the ones here were so outdated, but at least it was clean now.

I decided to start on the bedroom. The walls, once a creamy white, were now a patchy sepia colour. This seemed a good place to start. I had bought white paint for the doors and skirtings and a shade of cornflower blue for the walls. It seemed to me to be a restful colour, and that was something I needed, but how could I relax when there were people being murdered all around me? I looked around the bedroom. I would have to pull all that heavy furniture away from the walls, I could have done with Flynn's help with that, but my pride wouldn't allow me to ask him. I was strong, I could manage. I was keen to begin, so changed into a light T-shirt and my overalls, and prised the lid off the can of white paint. I had done half way along the first skirting board when the phone rang. It was Flynn.

'You're back. Why didn't you call me?' he sounded annoyed.

'I didn't want to bother you last night. You weren't exactly enthusiastic about my exploits,' I said defensively.

'Look Shannon, I just want to keep you out of trouble. Whoever sent that note means business!'

'You called me Shannon! Where did that come from?'

I heard him sigh at the other end of the phone, 'Her name's been on everyone's lips since you moved here. It was a slip of the tongue. Don't read anything into that please! Did you find out anything else yesterday?'

'Only that I had a twin who died soon after birth. So no

leads there.' I played it down for his benefit, although this information was the best I'd had yet. But I did tell him about my visit to the police station this morning.

'Damn it, Lee. I told you not to do that,' he yelled down the phone.

'You're not my keeper! I can make decisions for myself!' I yelled back, 'And I needed someone to take me seriously and support me over this.'

'Didn't I come all the way to Manchester with you? Wasn't that support enough?'

'Yes, and I'm very grateful. But I need to take this further, and I don't think you're with me over that.'

'What else have you done?' he said angrily, 'I hope you haven't been worrying Joseph Chase!'

'Of course not. I'm not that insensitive, especially after what happened to Mark.'

'Oh, you know about that?' he replied.

'I heard about it in the paint shop,' I informed him, 'And speaking of paint, I need to get back to my decorating. It's going to keep me busy for a few days.'

He seemed satisfied with this. If I was decorating I wouldn't be out sleuthing. I sometimes wished Flynn wasn't so protective, it wasn't as if we were engaged or anything. In fact we seemed to be getting further apart.

I went back to my painting.

Chapter 17

Joseph Chase sat under a garden parasol sipping an ice cold beer. It was a hot, humid afternoon, and he had no inclination to do anything else. He was still processing the events of the previous evening, it was impossible to think of the firm without Mark. He had been the nearest thing Joseph had to a son, and they had become very close, especially since Shannon had died. But however bad Joseph was feeling, Andrew must be feeling ten times worse! He'd lost his only child, his son and heir.

Chris sauntered out into the garden, a glass of whisky in his hand.

'Well, Uncle Joseph, this is a sad state of affairs,' he said, sitting down under the parasol.

Joseph nodded, 'Indeed, yes. Mark will be missed, and not only by the company.'

'So perhaps you'll agree to me taking over the Winterbourne project now. We can't just let it sit there, and no one else has worked on the project as I have. There's no one better qualified to take over, and you know it.'

'Nothing's changed as far as I'm concerned, Chris. This is an ethical company. The out-of-town site has been approved and that's where the building will take place. Any decisions about who takes over from Mark will be down to Andrew. In fact Andrew will be at the helm for quite a while. I've decided to sell my shares in the company.'

This was not how this interview was supposed to go. Chris swallowed the rest of his whisky in one gulp, 'Why would you do that, uncle? You and Andrew started this company and made it big! Why give up on it now?'

'I'm an old man, Chris, as you pointed out so blatantly in my office. I've lost my wife, my daughter and now Mark. I don't have the interest or the inclination to go on. I shall offer Andrew my shares, but my guess is he will be of a similar mind to me. They would then be floated on the open market.'

'You don't need to do this. I could run that company as well as anybody. Just give me a chance!'

'My decision is final. One way or another the shares will be sold. I can leave it to Andrew to see that the buyer retains the ethics we believe in. Chase/Colbourne will remain a community minded company.'

'I don't think so,' Chris pulled the letter out of his pocket and handed it to his uncle.

Joseph's blood pressure rose as he read, realising that Chris must have been snooping around in his private papers. He was right not to trust him.

'So, do I get to take over the project, or would you like the world to see just how ethical you really are?'

Joseph put the letter down on the table and glared at his nephew, 'Get out! I won't give in to blackmail. Now give me your keys and get out of my house!'

Chris slammed the keys down on the table, turned and walked back through the house, knowing he'd never set foot in it again. But he wasn't beaten yet. He could still ruin his uncle by publishing the contents of the letter.

He got in his car and rang Kelsey. She would know what to do to turn this situation around. Joseph might have won this battle, but he hadn't won the war!

* * * * *

DCI Hutton and DS Halliday were the second lot of visitors Joseph had that day. They found him still in the garden, the sun having moved round leaving the patio set in complete shade.

'Mr Chase, sorry to bother you again so soon, but if

you could spare us a few minutes?' Hutton thought the old man seemed to have aged overnight.

Joseph looked up at them, 'You better sit down.'

The officers sat, glad to be in the shade. The sun was still beating down and there was no cooling breeze to ease the intensity of it. There was no movement in the air at all.

Hutton took out a handkerchief and wiped the sweat from his brow, 'Mr Chase, I know this is bad timing, but could you tell us about your daughter, Shannon? How did you find out about her death?'

The old man's face crumpled and he ran a hand over it, 'Shannon. Why do you want to know about her? She was the best daughter I could have had. Beautiful, intelligent, she ran the international side of the company. She had a degree in languages. She and Mark were being primed to take over the company when Andrew and I retired. But now……..,'

'Can you tell us about Shannon's death? If it's not too painful.'

Joseph sighed, a pained look on his face, 'There was an accident. She fell over the balcony – oh, not this one. We lived just outside Manchester, it happened there. Chris found her in the early hours of the morning, he'd been at a friend's birthday party, and got home about 2.45 in the morning. He saw her lying there, under the balcony. She suffered head injuries, she wouldn't have stood a chance.'

'She was your only child?' Halliday said.

Joseph nodded, 'We couldn't have any more. And I didn't want more. Shannon was enough. Of course if we'd known what was going to happen we might have thought differently, *an heir and a spare* as the saying goes, but after she died, we placed all our hopes on Mark.'

'What about your nephew, Christopher Chase? He works for you, doesn't he?' Hutton asked.

'Not any more,' Joseph said wistfully, 'I've recently

discovered Christopher isn't to be trusted. He hasn't got the interest of the firm at heart. In fact he seems determined to ruin the company.'

'How did he get on with Mark?' asked Halliday, 'Joanna suggested last night there was some rivalry between them?'

'They were all right at first. Chris joined the company straight from university at the request of his father, my late brother. But recently there has been a conflict of interests over an important contract, the Winterbourne project. You may have heard of it. They want to build on Spraggan's Meadow. It's a nature reserve and there is an alternative site further out of town. Okay, we might not make as much money if we build there, but at least we'll have done our bit for the environment. Is that all, inspector? I'm very tired.'

'Just one more thing, Mr Chase. Tell us all you know about the Helen Rosewell Maternity Home.'

Chapter 18

Lee

I had run out of paint. The pale blue had not covered the walls with just one coat, I should have bought a bigger tin. Now I would need another trip to the hardware store.

The town seemed quieter today, perhaps the oppressive heat was keeping people indoors in the cool. I felt a trickle of sweat roll down my face. I caught a glimpse of my reflection in a shop window, paint-splashed overalls, hair tied back in an untidy ponytail, no make-up. But who makes up their face to do the decorating?

Had I known I was going to bump into Sergeant Halliday I might have made more of an effort.

He was coming towards me as I neared the car park, hopefully I would be able to hide in the car till he'd gone by, but he was making a beeline straight for me.

'Miss Filmer. You've saved me a trip, I was on my way to see you.'

'Oh, hello sergeant. I came out for a tin of paint,' I said, stating the obvious.

'Well, I don't need to be a detective to work that one out,' he replied with a grin, 'I've got some news, I'd rather not talk in the street, do you fancy a coffee?'

I was gasping for a drink. 'That would be great,' I answered, 'but nowhere posh as I'm not exactly dressed for morning coffee!'

'You look fine,' he said, as I unlocked my car and stood the paint can on the floor.

Ten minutes later we were sipping cappuccinos in the café. I was conscious of my paint-stained overalls. Had he not been so smartly dressed in a suit and tie, we might just have got away with looking like two workpeople on a coffee break.

'You were right about Shannon Chase,' he began, 'She was adopted as a small baby, and she was your twin.'

'So she didn't die in that maternity hospital,' I said, 'But if she recovered, why weren't my parents told? I know they weren't expecting two babies, but I'm sure they would have wanted us both once we were born.'

'This is where it gets complicated,' the sergeant went on, 'Joseph and Isla Chase were not able to have children of their own. Joseph was a powerful figure in the community and had a lot of sway with notable people in those days, including some of the doctors at the Helen Rosewell Maternity Hospital.

One of those doctors was later convicted of baby farming and struck off the medical register. Joseph had paid him a substantial amount of money in exchange for a child. Your mother had only been expecting to take one baby home so if this second baby 'died' your parents would be none the worse off. But Joseph was not satisfied with just obtaining a baby in this way, he wanted a piece of the action, he needed to keep his business afloat, it was early days then, he could easily have gone under. Chase/Colbourne wasn't the huge concern it is today. So he teamed up with the doctor and provided him with names of couples desperate for a child and prepared to pay handsomely for it. And got a good payoff himself.'

I gulped my coffee, 'Baby farming! My parents had another child they never got to know! I never expected anything like that!'

But had I? The agency nurse brought in to take care of sick babies had seemed strange to me when I'd first learned about it. Always the same nurse too. She was obviously in on the scam. I repeated all this to the sergeant who listened closely, something Flynn had never done!

'The Chase's only redeeming factor is that they were good parents,' the sergeant went on, 'Joseph adored Shannon, and still grieves for her. If this story breaks he'll be ruined. He runs an ethical company, or so it appears. But we will be looking into his business practices, though I'm sure we won't find anything untoward. With his past he'll have kept his nose clean since then.'

'Did Shannon know?' I asked.

'She was never told.'

'And she died at the family home in Manchester?'

'Yes, Christopher Chase found her lying beneath the balcony she had fallen from when he got back home from a party. We will be seeing him soon to confirm Joseph's statement.'

'And Joseph admitted all this' I asked.

He nodded, 'Reluctantly. But he knew we were on the right track. He decided to come clean so he could get his version of the facts in before anyone else did.'

'One thing puzzles me, Sergeant Halliday. The house I told you about in Manchester. I felt drawn to it, and then I had that flashback of falling. How could I have had a flashback about something that happened to someone else?'

'I'm no expert, but twins often feel pain when the other one is hurting. It's not unusual.'

I had to accept that explanation - there wasn't any other.

'So that house I saw was Shannon's family home?'

'Actually, no. We're still trying to find out who it belonged to at that time, the Chases lived about three miles away from that house.'

'And the doctor? What happened to him?'

'He served his sentence and was killed in a car accident shortly after he got out.'

'So as far as I'm concerned, the case is closed?'

'Not quite. We still have the murders of Eve Pritchard and Mark Colbourne to solve. Inspector Hutton thinks there is a link to you, but we're not sure what it is.'

'So if I hadn't moved here, these people might still be alive.'

It was a distressing thought that my actions had caused the deaths of two people.

The sergeant looked at me sternly, 'You were in no way responsible for their deaths. That's totally down to the person who committed these crimes. I'll keep you up to date with our enquiries, but in the meantime be careful. We still don't know who sent you those letters.'

The letters! I'd forgotten all about them. There hadn't been any more and no one had tried to physically harm me, so I'd pushed them to the back of my mind.

'Would you like more coffee?' he asked.

'No, I'm fine. Thank you. I should be getting back, I've got walls to paint,' I said, smiling at him.

He walked me back to the car and we talked about mundane things, the weather, the drought that was going on in the rivers and streams. It felt natural to be walking alongside him.

'Thank you for the coffee, sergeant,' I said as I unlocked the car.

'You're welcome, and it's Paul. At least when I'm off duty.'

'Lee,' I answered, getting into the car and fastening the seat belt.

He leaned into the car as I went to turn on the ignition, 'Perhaps we could do this again sometime, but please check you haven't got a large blob of blue paint on your chin first!'

I glanced in the mirror and felt my face reddening. I wouldn't be going out without make-up again!

Chapter 19

Frank Hutton sat in Stephanie Lang's sitting room drinking tea. Stephanie sat with her foot on a footstool, her leg plastered up to the knee.

'So, is it still painful?' Frank asked.

'Not so much now. It's just annoying me that I can't get around. I've got used to the crutches, they're fine until I need to get upstairs. Thank heavens I've got a downstairs loo!'

Stephanie's house was modern, all chrome and glass. Her sofa was like something out of a sci-fi movie, but it was very comfortable Frank noted as he sank back into it. The furniture was all black and white painted units. The laminate flooring was ash grey, and white slatted blinds covered the windows. The only colour in the room was a vase of bright orange flowers on the coffee table.

'Netta sends her love,' said Frank.

Stephanie smiled, she and Frank's wife had been good friends since she had become Frank's sergeant a few years ago.

'And how is my godson?' she asked. Stephanie adored the little boy and had been thrilled when she was asked to be his godmother.

'Robbie's doing fine. He's all over the place now he can walk. I'll get Netta to bring him over while you're off work – if you can stand the mess he seems to create!'

She nodded, 'And how's my replacement getting on?'

'Actually, he's okay. He works a little differently than we're used to, but he gets the job done. I wouldn't be surprised if he makes inspector by the time he's thirty.'

'Ambitious then,' Stephanie said wistfully, 'Well, I won't be back for at least a month, so make the most of him!'

'He's good, Steph, but I'll be glad to see you back.'

'Well, if there's anything I can do? I gather you're still working on the Pritchard murder?'

'That and Mark Chase now.'

'Yes, I heard about that. But as I said, if there's anything I can help with? My legs don't work but my brain's still functioning as well as ever.'

'Your take on this would be much appreciated, Steph. Okay, here we go! We've got Lee Filmer who turns out to be Shannon Chase's twin sister, and Joseph and Isla Chase were not Shannon's natural parents. Eve Pritchard is murdered after mistaking Lee for Shannon, then Mark is killed by running off the road after someone cuts his brake cables. Lee is the link between these events, but we don't know how or why. She had an accident herself four years ago and can't remember a thing except flashbacks of Shannon falling over a balcony, but she was miles away at the time, in a coma on the highway. Now she is receiving anonymous letters. So if you've got anything to add to that, fire away!'

Stephanie adjusted her foot on the footstool, 'It must be something to do with the company, Chase/Colbourne. With both Mark and Shannon out of the picture, who's next in line? Who inherits?'

'The only relative connected to the company is Christopher Chase, Joseph's nephew, but there's been some sort of an altercation between him and Joseph, and it appears Joseph's severed all ties with him.'

'Then perhaps we should be looking for someone outside the company. Who would benefit from Mark being out of the way?'

'That's a good point, Steph. The disagreement between Joseph and Christopher began over the Winterbourne project. Then to add fuel to the fire Mark got promoted onto the board of directors and Christopher bitterly resented that. Christopher is all for going along with Emmerson's proposition for the Winterbourne project, but it's not the ethical one Mark had planned. Freddie Emmerson is also the father of Christopher Chase's girlfriend, Kelsey.'

'I know her,' Stephanie said, 'Very pushy young woman, used to getting her own way. Can't say I like her very much, but I've heard she has a good head for business.'

'Mmm,' murmured Frank, 'There might be something there. Worth checking out. I'll send Halliday over there tomorrow. But I still don't see why anyone would want to get rid of Lee Filmer. Unless they didn't know she was Shannon's twin and thought Shannon had returned to wreak havoc on their plans. If Shannon was back she'd be first in line for the inheritance.'

'That was exactly what Eve Pritchard thought – that Lee actually was Shannon, even though she knew Shannon had been dead for four years. So who else would be likely to think the same way?'

'The family seem to think Christopher Chase was responsible for Mark's death. His nose was put out of joint when Mark joined the board of directors and his own application was blackballed. But he categorically denies murder.'

'Well, he would do, wouldn't he? I've yet to come across a murderer who was willing to admit his crime when asked' Stephanie said with a wry smile. 'What is your opinion of Christopher?'

'I was inclined to believe him. Don't know why, he's not a particularly likeable chap.'

'So I've heard. But anyone who takes up with Kelsey Emmerson isn't likely to win a popularity contest. Have you met her?'

'Briefly, when we went there to check out Yvonne Whitmore's alibi. She claimed she and Kelsey were talking outside the tea tent when Eve was killed.'

'And Kelsey confirmed that' Stephanie said, thoughtfully, 'And Kelsey is obviously backing her father's proposition for the Winterbourne project.'

Frank nodded, 'Of course she is. That's why we're going to take a closer look at that young lady. She'll do anything to get that site on Spraggan's Meadow.'

'Even murder?'

'Cant discount it' Frank replied drily.

'So if this building site turns out to be an entirely separate issue from the murders, what else have you got?'

'Sod all, Steph. Sod all!'

Frank looked at his watch, 'I'd better get going. Just popped round to see how you were doing.'

He stood up to leave, 'Take care of that ankle, Steph. Catch you soon.'

'Bye, Frank. Thank Netta for the chocolates.'

Stephanie sank back in her chair after Frank had gone, wishing she was back at work. She missed her colleagues at the station, and she missed the excitement her work brought. She liked nothing better than solving mysteries, and the case her boss was working on sounded intriguing. But Frank had a new sergeant now, and a good one by the sound of it. She hoped he wouldn't get too comfortable at Barling. She wanted her job back!

Chapter 20

Lee

I was painting again, the bathroom this time, when the phone rang. It was Flynn, he had an uncanny knack of ringing when I was half way through painting a skirting board.

'Lee, I haven't heard from you in ages. Are you all right?'

'I'm fine, Flynn. Busy decorating the cottage. I haven't been out much lately.'

'We should meet up. How about a drink in the Green Dragon tonight?'

'I don't know, Flynn. I'm not sure it's a good idea. We're really not on the same wavelength any more, are we?'

I sensed the annoyance in his voice, 'Just because I don't go along with all your ideas doesn't mean I've stopped caring. For heaven's sake, we can still be friends, can't we?'

Put like that, it did seem a bit churlish not to see him. If Barling was going to be my permanent home, I couldn't avoid bumping into him in the normal course of events. Flynn wasn't someone I would want to make an enemy of.

'Okay,' I answered, 'What time shall I meet you?'

'I'll pick you up at 7.30.'

'I'd rather walk,' I told him, 'It's not far and I really need some fresh air after being indoors all week.'

He grudgingly agreed. If I was going to see Flynn again it was going to be on my terms this time.

I left the cottage just before 7.30. It was a pleasant evening, cooler now after the heat of the day. I wore a summer dress with a light linen jacket, and despite my earlier misgivings about going out I was actually looking forward to an evening away from the cottage.

I got to the Green Dragon before Flynn. I got myself a beer and sat down at a table to wait. The pub was old, the original beams still propped up the ceiling and old fashioned lamps stood in the window sills, just for the ambience; they were never lit. A couple of elderly men propped up the bar and one or two people were sitting at tables with their drinks. I hoped Flynn wasn't going to be long – sitting around in pubs on my own was not something I would normally do.

He came rushing in about ten minutes later. 'Sorry, Lee. I got caught up. I was afraid you'd have given up on me and gone home.'

'It's okay, I've not been here long and I was just soaking up the atmosphere. It's the first time I've been out of the house in days.'

He seemed pleased to hear that, 'How's the decorating going?' he asked, taking off his jacket and throwing it over a chair.

That was good - we were on safe ground, 'It's going well. Bedroom finished and bathroom underway. It's good to get out of my grubby overalls and dress up for a change'

He got himself a drink and we sat chatting amicably. I wasn't going to mention Shannon or Manchester. I figured we might just get through the evening if we avoided certain subjects.

But Flynn had other ideas. 'How's the sleuthing going?' he asked.

I took a sip of my drink, 'I'm leaving it to the police,' I answered, 'Now I know for sure who I am, I'm hoping things will quieten down.'

'What about the anonymous letter? Have you found out

who it was from?'

'No, but I'm being careful not to get in anyone's way, I don't know why someone should want me out of the way. But whoever sent it must know by now that I'm not Shannon, therefore no longer a threat to them.'

'Why would you be a threat?'

'Well, someone didn't want me around, did they? And the only reason could be that they thought I was Shannon, and they didn't want her around either!'

'Okay, so Eve Pritchard mistook you for Shannon. But that's all been explained. She was your twin, identical twins look the same. Maybe what's been happening at Joseph Chase's house is unconnected with you after all. Coincidences do happen.'

'I don't want to talk about it any more,' I said, desperate to get him off the subject, 'Tell me something about yourself. I know you're an engineer, but who do you work for?'

'I'm self employed,' he replied, 'I go where there's work. At the moment I'm with a company in the construction business. Emmerson's, you might have heard of it? Now who was that guy you were with in town the other day? It didn't look like a date, you were covered in paint!'

So he was good at changing the subject too! I leaned back in my seat and took a swig of my drink, 'It wasn't a date. It was the police sergeant who's been working on my case. He doesn't believe in fantasies, we're dealing with facts here,' I couldn't resist adding. So Flynn had been in town that day I met Paul Halliday and went for a coffee. I hadn't seen him, why hadn't he made himself known? Surely that would have been the natural thing to do? It felt like he had been watching me, keeping tabs, and that was not a comfortable feeling!

Flynn picked up a beer mat and started turning it over and over on the table, 'Okay, perhaps I was a bit hasty in dismissing your claims, but I was only trying to stop you getting into trouble. You're right to leave it to the police. Don't go poking about in things you don't understand.'

I kept silent. I wasn't sure if that was a warning or if Flynn really was concerned for my safety.

'What have I said now?' he asked, a look of exasperation on his face, 'Okay, I made a hash of things. What do you want me to do to prove I believe you now?'

'If you really want to help, there is one thing you can do – Get me an interview with Joseph Chase!'

* * * * *

The following morning Joseph Chase's photo leapt out at me from the newspaper, under the headline:

'Ethical' Tycoon in Baby Farming Scandal!

I read on. It was all there, including a picture of the Helen Rosewell Maternity Home. How the hell did this get out? I hadn't even told Flynn, and the police wouldn't have talked to the press, not in the middle of an enquiry.

It was early but I decided to ring Paul. He answered on the first ring, 'Lee, I was just about to ring you. Have you seen the paper?'

'It's what I'm ringing about. How can this have happened?'

'Who else knew about this?' Paul asked.

'I have no idea, but someone did. Someone here who has it in for Joseph Chase. Maybe the Colbournes knew about it. They're very close to Joseph, and they were around at the time of Shannon's adoption.'

'I'm going to see them later today. Look, are you free this evening? We could meet for a drink, to discuss the case of course.'

'8 o'clock in the Green Dragon?' I suggested, 'Paul, I can't help thinking this is all my fault. If I hadn't come to Barling, looking the image of my twin sister, maybe none of this would have happened. I seem to have opened the biggest can of worms in Christendom!'

'Lee, none of this is down to you. You weren't to know any of this was going to happen. This baby farming thing was bound to come out sooner or later. They were lucky it didn't come out before now. And if someone chose to murder two people, that's down to them, not you.'

That made me feel a bit better. We ended the call just as I heard someone rattle the letter box. On the hall floor was another note:

'GO BACK TO MANCHESTER. YOU ARE IN DANGER HERE!'

I yanked the front door open just in time to see a small boy cycling off down the road. 'Hey, you!' I yelled after him. Surprisingly he stopped and waited for me to run down the road to meet him.

'You just put this through my door,' I said, waving the note at him, 'Who asked you to do that?'

'A lady. She gave me a couple of quid. Easy money.'

'What did she look like? Was she young or old?'

'Didn't really notice. She had a big sunhat on. Couldn't see much of her face.'

'Have you ever seen her before? This is important.'

'Never seen her before in my life. Now can I go?'

I went back indoors, and read the note again. There was something different about it. This wasn't so much a threat but a warning of danger. Could my anonymous letter writer possibly be on my side? This was getting more mysterious by the minute. And the writer knew I came from Manchester!

There was nothing I could do, so I went back to painting the bathroom. It was nearly finished, I'd mixed what was left of the blue with some white emulsion and created a 'white with a hint of blue' shade. With the grey bathroom suite and the white tiles that I'd freshly grouted, it looked quite good, fresher and lighter.

The day passed quickly and I showered and dressed

ready to meet Paul, this time with make-up and no paint smudges!

He was there before me, dressed casually in light slacks and a dark blue shirt, open at the neck.

'I've got you a beer,' he said as I sat down, 'Hope that's okay?'

'Just what I need,' I replied

'So, how has your day been?' he asked.

'Strange,' I answered, 'First I had a row with Flynn on the phone, and then this appeared.'

I showed him the note and he agreed with me, it did appear to be warning me of danger, not threatening me with it.

'What about this guy, Flynn?' Paul said, 'You told me he was over-protective.'

I thought about it for only a moment, 'No. Flynn wouldn't be subtle. He'd come right out and tell me if I was in danger. Actually, that's more or less what he's been doing all the time. And he was genuinely surprised when the first note arrived. And that boy said it was a woman who paid him to deliver this one.'

'That's not particularly significant,' he answered, 'He could have got anyone to pass the note to the boy. But the likelihood of that happening is low. Whoever's doing this would want to involve as few people as possible.'

He paused to take a sip of his beer, 'So we're likely looking for a woman. Have you got close to any women since you've been here?'

'No one really, the only one I've spoken to was Eve Pritchard, and I wasn't very friendly towards her. I regret that now.'

'I'm sure she would have understood. I have some news for you about the house you visited, where you had your flashback. It was owned by a widow named Edith Berry. Does the name mean anything to you?'

I shook my head, 'I don't know anyone of that name. Is

she still alive?'

'Unfortunately not. The place was sold after she died and I believe it's been sold on again since.'

'So I had a flashback of an incident I never experienced, at a place I've never visited, and I can't remember any of it. Just great!'

'Yeah, there has to be a logical explanation and we will find it. Don't give up hope.'

That was easier said than done, but he was right, I had to see this through, if only to get justice for Eve Pritchard and Mark Colbourne.

* * * * *

Andrew and Elizabeth Colbourne were in Andrew's company office, when his secretary ushered in Hutton and Halliday.

'Inspector Hutton,' Andrew, seated at his desk, looked up from his paperwork. Elizabeth stood by the printer.

'Mr Colbourne,' Hutton began, 'We have a few more questions. I'm assuming you've read the papers this morning. Did you know about Joseph Chase's involvement with the baby farming ring at the time?'

'We knew about Shannon's adoption,' Andrew said, 'I suspected money had changed hands, the adoption came up too quickly to have gone through the normal channels, but I never questioned Joseph. I figured it was his private business. How did all this get out, inspector?'

Hutton ignored the question, 'Did you ever have reason to visit the Helen Rosewell Maternity Home?'

Elizabeth turned round, 'Mark was born there. I never had a second child so we had no reason to go back again.'

'Before you left Manchester, were you aware of a house just outside the city called Hilltops? It was owned by a Mrs Edith Berry.'

Andrew shook his head, 'Doesn't ring any bells. Is this

place significant, inspector?'

'It's just part of our enquiries,' Hutton told him, 'Now, Joseph's nephew, Christopher Chase, what's your opinion of him?'

'A most disagreeable young man!' said Elizabeth.

'And you, sir?' Hutton asked Andrew.

'As Elizabeth said, not an easy young man to like. Christopher is ambitious, wants to run before he can walk. He was very envious of Mark, even as a child. Mark was always out in front, but that's because he wasn't afraid of hard work. Chris tends to sit back and take the credit for the work done by other people.'

'How well do you know his girlfriend, Kelsey Emmerson?'

'All I'm going to say about that is that they're well suited!'

'What Andrew means is that she's a money grabbing little madam who will stop at nothing to get what she wants,' Elizabeth said, shaking her head, 'She'll never marry Chris. She's using him for some purpose of her own, and the Lord knows what that is! When he's of no further use to her she'll drop him like a hot brick.'

'How about Kelsey's father, what can you tell us about him?'

'Huh!' Andrew grunted, 'Freddie Emmerson! Freddie's had some luck where business is concerned, inspector. We were all based in and around Manchester till the new industrial units went up in Dengate, we all moved down here about the same time. Then Freddie's luck changed. His wife, Dorothy took an overdose, and now it's rumoured his business is in trouble. He's relying on getting the contract with Chase/Colbourne to keep him afloat. If the Winterbourne project doesn't go ahead, it's likely he'll go bankrupt.'

'When did his wife die, Mr Colbourne?' Hutton asked.

'Soon after they got here. There had been some trouble in Manchester and she suffered with anxiety.

They came here for a fresh start, but she couldn't handle it.'

'This trouble. Do you know what it was?'

'He was closer to Joseph at the time, Isla was a nurse and she was helping Dorothy with her nerves. I shouldn't wonder if he wasn't tied up in this baby farming thing too.'

'What's happening with the Winterbourne project now that Mark's no longer at the helm?' asked Halliday.

Andrew sighed, 'We're still pushing ahead with it. We're not giving in to Freddie's demands to build on Spraggan's Meadow. Now more than ever, we have to show the people that we are environmentally motivated. If Emmerson wants the contract he'll have to agree to the out of town site. I owe it to Mark to carry on what he started.'

'Thank you, Mr Colbourne, Mrs Colbourne. Oh, by the way, have either of you met Lee Filmer?'

'That girl who looks like Shannon? I've seen her around the town, but we've never met her,' said Elizabeth, moving away from the printer and standing by her husband at his desk.

'You might like to know she's Shannon's twin,' was Hutton's parting shot. He noticed the look of consternation on Elizabeth's face as he and Halliday took their leave.

'So Isla Chase was a nurse' Hutton commented on exiting the building, 'What are the chances she was the 'agency' nurse brought in to take care of the sick babies?'

'That's what went through my mind' Halliday replied. 'Lee said she spoke to a nurse who was there at the time of her birth. Hopefully she will remember if Isla Chase ever worked there. But it's unlikely. This Sally would know Joseph's wife surely?'

'Maybe, but check it out anyway. Apparently the nurse was only brought in on those occasions when there was a child suitable for adoption. My guess is the child would have 'died' fairly soon after the nurse's arrival, she wouldn't have been there long enough to form a bond with any of the regular nurses. She may not even have been a nurse at all'

'Joseph was open with us when we finally got him talking, why wouldn't he have told us if Isla was involved? She's been dead a while so it wouldn't have hurt her.'

'Human nature is a funny thing, Halliday. Joseph may have been happy enough to deprive natural parents of their babies, but he'd do anything to preserve his wife's good name. He doted on her and Shannon.'

Back at the station Halliday rang the Rosewell Maternity Home and spoke to Sally Tate.

'No, sergeant' Sally told him, 'I knew Isla well. She used to come in and help with the babies on a voluntary basis after she gave up working at the hospital. And she was really a psychiatric nurse. She loved being with the babies, but of course once she adopted Shannon we didn't see so much of her.'

'Have you any idea who this agency nurse was?' Halliday asked

'No, we knew her only as Dotty.'

'Do you know where she is now?'

'I heard she was dead, sergeant, as are most people connected to this case. I have to go now, duty calls. Please give my regards to Lee.'

Halliday rang off. Another dead end! Isla Chase had not been involved in the scandal. He was glad about that but had no idea why.

Chapter 21

Hutton and Halliday left the offices of Emmerson and Co, where they had just interviewed Freddie Emmerson, who was not pleased at the intrusion.

'What do you want, inspector? I'm a busy man and I've got nothing to do with the murders of Mark Colbourne or that Pritchard woman!'

'It's about another matter we want to talk to you about,' Hutton informed him, 'You must have seen the papers, so you will know that Joseph Chase is currently being investigated for baby farming. You knew the Chase family when you all lived in Manchester. I believe your late wife was friendly with Isla Chase?'

'Dorothy was ill. Isla was helping her, or trying to! But that's as far as the friendship went. After Dorothy died there was no reason to remain in contact with Isla.'

'But you and Joseph remained friends?'

'Business associates, inspector. Just business associates.'

'But you were friends once?'

'A long time ago, inspector. Chase cut me out of more than one good deal. Any liaison I have with him now is strictly business.'

'But you continue to work with him? I'm surprised.'

'If it's mutually beneficial to us both, then yes. But I'm watching his back all the time.'

'And the Winterbourne project, you'll be working with Chase/Colbourne again over that. I heard the future of your own company rests on this project?'

'I don't know where you heard that, inspector. The Winterbourne project would certainly be a feather in our cap, but if we don't secure the contract we'll survive.'

'I understand your daughter is engaged to Joseph's nephew, Christopher.'

'Yes, sir! Chris is okay, a bit of a wet blanket sometimes, but I guess Kelsey knows what she's doing.'

'No sign of a wedding yet then?'

'Doesn't look like it. Chris is keen, it's Kelsey who keeps stalling.'

'So Kelsey, Mark, Chris and Shannon Chase all grew up together in Manchester?' said Hutton.

'Kelsey didn't have much to do with them as children. She only got to know them as she grew up. The other three were close though.'

'Did you know about Joseph's activities in baby farming at the time?' Hutton asked.

'No, like I said, I didn't have a lot to do with them apart from work. I certainly wouldn't know what went on in his private life. But nothing would surprise me where Joseph Chase is concerned!'

'The Colbournes hinted that there had been some trouble, which possibly contributed to your wife's death. Could you elaborate on that please?'

'There was no trouble! We were struggling to get keep the business afloat. Who isn't these days! It was a stressful time for all of us. Dorothy was the sort to worry about everything, she suffered acute depression just before she died. I thought the change of scenery would be good for her when we moved down here, but if anything she got worse.'

'Just one last question, sir, Are you familiar with a house called Hilltops? Perhaps it was your family home?'

'No, inspector, It was not my home. I never lived there.'

Hutton looked at him full in the face, 'But you knew who did.'

Chapter 22

Lee

Unbelievable! I had just started painting the hall when the phone rang. It was Flynn.

'Do you have a built in radar where paint and skirting boards are concerned?' I asked jokingly.

He laughed, 'No, but I think you'll be pleased at the interruption. I've done as you asked and got you an audience with Joseph Chase. Tonight at 9 pm.'

'Oh, why so late?'

'Well, I expected a better reaction than that!' He sounded disgruntled

'I am grateful, Flynn. I wasn't expecting it so soon, if at all. I'm just surprised he agreed to see me. Hasn't he been taken away by the police over that baby scam thing though?'

'He was, but he's not been charged with anything yet. They had to let him go.'

'Oh, okay. I'll be there at 9 tonight then.'

'It's not that simple, Lee. One of the conditions to him agreeing to see you was that I go with you. He's never met you and looking so much like his dead daughter I don't know how he's going to react. I'll pick you up just before 9 tonight.'

He put the phone down before I had time to say anything more, but I wasn't going to argue. He'd done what I wanted, and nothing was going to stop me meeting the man who had adopted - no, - bought my sister.

I had to find a way to fill the hours till I finally got to meet Joseph Chase. The painting had lost its appeal, my mind was no longer on the decorating, but I couldn't leave it half done so I pressed on. As I painted I went over in my mind all the questions I wanted to ask him about my sister, all the things this man could tell me, things I would have known if he hadn't stolen her away from her rightful family! He had deprived not only my parents of knowing their daughter, but also had deprived me of my sister! Sisters had a special bond, so I'd been told, but Shannon was dead so I would never get to find out what that would have been like. I wasn't sure I would ever forgive him for that!

Flynn arrived dead on the dot of 8.45. He was dressed casually, in jeans and a T-shirt. I also wore jeans, but with a thin jumper, the evenings were getting chillier as we approached the autumn.

I was nervous of meeting Joseph, I wasn't sure what I was going to say this man, now a criminal in the eyes of the law. Part of me rebelled at the thought of even being in the same room as him, but this was the only way I was going to get to know Shannon myself - through the memories of the man she had always known as her father.

The sun was setting as we pulled up, way back from the house. It looked imposing in the evening shadows and I shivered, feeling a touch apprehensive as we got out of the car. There was another car parked further up the road, and a tall, slim blonde girl got out of it and started down the road towards us.

She looked vaguely familiar, but I couldn't place where or even if I had seen her before. As she got nearer, I could see a smirk on her face, which made me feel uncomfortable.

Flynn firmly grasped my arm, leading me towards her.

'You don't mind if Kelsey joins us, do you?' he asked.

Kelsey. The name sounded familiar. Then I remembered, she was Christopher Chase's girlfriend. I'd heard Paul mention her. But what was she doing here? This was supposed to be my time with Joseph. I'd agreed to Flynn being present, but I certainly did not want this girl around while I questioned him.

'Hi there,' she said, giving Flynn a peck on the cheek. They obviously knew each other better than I thought.

'So this is Lee,' she said, looking me up and down, 'Well come on. Let's get on with it.'

She flounced off, Flynn and I following, not to the front door as I expected, but round to the back of the house.

The back garden was stunning. There was a wide herringbone patterned patio complete with a luxury set of patio furniture, which looked inviting after such a sultry day. I could imagine relaxing out there after the heat of the day with a long, cool drink. The path leading down to the end of the garden was flanked by topiary bay trees and conifers. The flower beds were immaculate and there was a central water feature, a fountain of cherubs pouring the water from pitchers. The overall effect was like a smaller version of gardens you see attached to stately homes.

I slowed my pace to marvel at the spectacle, dragging Flynn back with me as he still gripped my arm tightly. Kelsey looked round, annoyed at the dalliance, 'Come on' she said impatiently, 'We haven't got all night!'

Reluctantly I turned towards the house, wondering why I felt so reluctant to go in, I would have been content to just sit out in the garden and interview Joseph there. Suddenly the house seemed dark and forbidding.

'Chris asked the old man to leave the back door unlocked for us' Kelsey said, opening the door and stepping inside. We stepped into a kind of scullery, a washing machine took pride of place, and there was an old stone sink with a washboard. A mix of old and new, but somehow it worked.

She led us through to a huge modern kitchen, nothing retro here. The units looked as if they'd just come out of a designer magazine, they were white, the floor tiles white and black, and every kitchen appliance imaginable adorned the granite worktops.

'Wow!' I said, looking around, 'What I'd give for a kitchen like this!'

Kelsey smirked, as if to say this is way beyond your means. But of course she was right. I didn't fit in with all this luxury.

'Through here,' Flynn said, still grasping my arm. He could let go now, I wasn't going to run away!

We followed Kelsey into a grand hall, with several doors. She opened one and led us into a sitting room.

This was also furnished exquisitely, deep pile carpet, antique furniture, and the largest TV screen I'd ever seen. I had a slight feeling of déjà vu, but the feeling quickly passed. I had seen rooms like this in glossy magazines, usually accompanied by the type of garden I had just walked through. They all looked just like this, and that must have subconsciously triggered the feeling that I'd been here before. I had expected Joseph to be in here, but the room was empty.

Flynn went back into the hall and yelled up the staircase, but there was no answer.

'Let's try upstairs,' said Kelsey, 'I expect the silly old bugger's fallen asleep and forgotten all about us!'

'Shouldn't we wait down here?' I asked. It didn't seem right to go wandering about in someone else's house without their permission.

'Oh, he won't mind,' Kelsey said, 'It won't be the first time this has happened. Chris thinks the old man's going senile!'

Flynn was propelling me towards the staircase. I justified this by thinking that Joseph may have had a fall and was lying there unable to get help. He was elderly and lived here all alone, so if an accident had happened, maybe we should investigate.

The staircase was a grand affair, dividing into two as we got near the top. We took the left hand fork and walked along a wide corridor till Kelsey opened a door and stood back to let us through. 'In here,' she said. Flynn and I entered the room, and found ourselves in a huge bedroom, with French windows overlooking the front garden.

Here was yet another grand room. A huge oak bed dominated the room, the furniture was Regency style and floor-length heavy brocade curtains hung over the French windows. There was a portrait on the wall of a beautiful lady, it had to be Joseph's wife. I stood looking at it for a minute, something stirred in my mind, not exactly a memory, but I felt I had known this woman. Her eyes stared at me intently, as if she was trying to tell me something. Was this another 'Shannon' moment? If it was, it wasn't like the other flashbacks I'd experienced.

Paul's words came back to me about twins experiencing the same feelings at the same moment. I knew that to be true, but did it still work if one of the twins was dead? Was Shannon trying to come through to me from the grave? The thought made me shudder. I hadn't known her when she was alive, why would she want anything to do with me now?

'That's Isla, Joseph's wife,' Flynn informed me, 'He never got over her death.'

'She's very beautiful,' I answered, my eyes still fixed on the dark-haired woman in the portrait, 'She looks…motherly. Shannon was lucky.'

I turned away, 'It must have been hard for Joseph, losing his wife and then his daughter.'

'We reap what we sow,' Kelsey said. There was an edge to her voice that I didn't understand. Was she referring to the baby farming episode? She would have read about it in the morning paper, but how could something that happened all those years ago affect her now? She was a child at the time, and probably hadn't got to know the Chase children back then. But Kelsey made up her own rules! Anything could have happened to set her baying for Joseph's blood! If there was such a thing as a modern day vampire she would be the epitome of it!

She went to the French windows, opened them wide and went outside onto the balcony.

'Come out here,' she commanded, 'It's a beautiful evening, just look at the sunset!'

Flynn took a step forward, but I hung back. Me and balconies weren't a good mix! I didn't want to provoke another flashback!

'Come on, you two,' Kelsey turned round to us, 'You don't want to miss this.'

Flynn, still holding me by the arm propelled me out onto the balcony. I fought off the dizzy feeling and tried to concentrate on the sunset. The sun was very low in the sky now, but the sky was ablaze with vivid pink and orange. Kelsey was right, it was something not to be missed.

'I think we should go down now,' I said, trying to move back through the French windows. I felt Flynn's grip tighten, and realisation hit me like a thunderbolt!

'Joseph's not here, is he?' I said quietly.

'How very observant!' Kelsey mocked, 'It's just the three of us. We're going to have a little party of our own.'

The word party sparked something in my memory. Nothing tangible, just a faint stirring in my mind.

'Where is Joseph?' I asked breathlessly.

'Joseph did a bad thing,' Kelsey went on, 'And now it's payback time. You reap what you sow,' she repeated.

'The police will see justice is done,' I said, playing for time. I had no doubt in my mind what her intention was. What I didn't understand was why? How could Joseph's past crime have any bearing on Kelsey? She was brought up by her natural parents, she wasn't a 'bought' child. I hadn't done anything to upset her and as far as I knew, Shannon hadn't either. And what was Flynn's part in all this?

I looked up at Flynn who was still maintaining a solid

grip on my arm, 'You and Kelsey – there was something between you once wasn't there?'

Kelsey grinned maliciously, 'Who said it had ever stopped? You don't think Flynn was ever really serious about you, do you? I hated every minute he was with you!'

I was puzzled, 'Then why……….' He had not known of my existence until I suddenly descended on the Dengate area. Apart from looking like Shannon Chase I had been a complete stranger to him. So why had he singled me out and acted so possessively towards me, trying to control my every move, thwarting every lead I had when trying to track down my past? Why should it matter to him who I was or where I came from? This was connected with Shannon, of that I was sure, but what I didn't know was what her connection with Flynn and Kelsey was!

I had to get out of there, and fast! I knew now it was no use appealing to Flynn's better nature - if he had one! I had occasionally glimpsed the man behind the façade, the softer side of him. I had no doubt Kelsey was the force behind all this evil, but Flynn was going along willingly with everything she said. And now he was slowly pushing me towards the edge of the balcony. 'Flynn?' I looked questioningly into his eyes, not the sparkling deep blue eyes that I'd been attracted to in the first place, but cold, domineering eyes that seemed to burn right through to my very soul! There was no way I could rely on him to help me – I was on my own. But I would fight.

Suddenly my head seemed to clear, as I gazed in horror at the man I had believed was my friend.

'It was you, wasn't it?' His grip loosened, 'It was both of you on that balcony the night Shannon died. You pushed her and then looked over the balcony to watch her fall! Why, Flynn? What had she ever done to you?'

'So you do remember something!' said Kelsey, then turning to Flynn, 'Come on, Flynn. She knows too much. Let's get it done and get out of here!'

'Wait!' I knew I wasn't going to be able to escape, but my instincts were telling me to keep talking. 'Why did you kill Shannon? If you're going to kill me too you have nothing to lose by telling me what this is all about.'

It was Kelsey who answered although I was addressing Flynn.

'She was in our way. Mark too. And now you. It's nothing personal, although I couldn't say the same thing about Joseph. He did a bad thing and now he's going to pay. I want him to feel the pain he's caused me.' She spoke loudly and bitterly.

'Don't you think he felt the pain when Shannon died? And when he lost his wife? Don't you think he's suffered enough?'

'Nowhere near!' her eyes were evil, her face contorted with hatred. But even then her beauty shone through – no wonder Flynn was captivated.

I decided to appeal to him one last time, 'Flynn, can't you see this is wrong? She's got you where she wants you. Don't let her win!'

He looked at me, his face expressionless, 'It's too late, Lee. It's gone too far. You know about Shannon's accident, you know about Eve Pritchard. We can't let you go now.'

I tried again, I was desperate now but at least I would understand a bit more about why they were doing this, 'Okay. Eve Pritchard. Tell me about her. Why did she have to die too?'

'You know the answer to that. She recognised you, or thought she did. She was a blabbermouth. It wouldn't be long before she planted the seeds of doubt in other people's minds too. We couldn't let that happen, now could we?'

Kelsey reached into her pocket and extracted a small square paper packet which she had taken from the dashboard in Flynn's car.

'What's that?' I asked.

Flynn grinned, 'Guitar strings A,B,D, and two E's. The G string is missing. Last seen Eve Pritchard was wearing it as a necklace!'

I shuddered. That they had killed Eve was no longer in doubt. They had just admitted it, but I was here alone, and by the time I was found it would be too late!

'But Eve was innocent!' I protested, 'Couldn't you have just convinced her she was mistaken? And what did it matter if Shannon really had come back? What did you have to lose?'

Kelsey was silent for a moment, then spoke quietly, a complete reversal of her former rantings, 'Everything! We would lose everything! We've waited for this too long to let it go now. All the planning, all the waiting, it can't all be in vain, Shannon has to stay dead, where she belongs!'

'But I wasn't even part of this community then. I don't know anything!' I pleaded.

'But you would soon,' Flynn cut in, 'All that digging and probing into things that didn't concern you; I had to stop you before you did us some real damage!'

'I just wanted to find out about my past, discover who I really am! What was so wrong in that?'

'Exactly that, you stupid girl. Exactly that!'

I glanced at Kelsey who was leaning patiently against the railings, her arms crossed, as casually as if she was waiting for a bus. She was about to commit murder for the fourth time, yet was calmly watching with amusement as I pleaded with Flynn for my life.

'Flynn, I know she's the one who's behind all this. She's got you to the point where you'll do anything for her! She's using Christopher in exactly the same way..................'

Kelsey sprang to life, pushing herself away from the railings, her face contorted with hate, advancing towards me and screaming, 'Shut up! Shut up! You don't know anything! Flynn, do it now!'

There was the slightest hesitation on Flynn's part, then

Kelsey rushed towards me, knocking me off balance. I gripped the railings as I felt her hands on my shoulders, but the next second Flynn was there prising my fingers off the railings and lifting me towards the edge of the balcony. I fought, but it was two against one and Flynn was stronger than both of us.

I screamed and had my third and final flashback, except this time it was for real. There was nothing I could do to stop this happening and I felt myself falling, falling towards the ground, the wind making that familiar rushing sound in my ears. I felt my shoulder hit something hard, then there was a thud as I hit the ground. Then everything went black.

It was Paul's voice I heard when I came to, 'It's all right, Lee. We've got them. It's over.'

I was aware of a scuffle going on around me, and as my vision cleared, I saw the place was full of uniformed police. Inspector Hutton had Flynn in handcuffs and I heard him say, 'Flynn Wyatt, I'm arresting you for the murders of Eve Pritchard, Mark Chase and the attempted murder of Shannon Chase.......'

Attempted murder? I didn't understand, Shannon was already dead. They pushed her off the balcony and Christopher found her when he got home from that party. I paused, there it was again. The party! There was something significant about this party. My head hurt, and I gave up trying to remember.

Chapter 23

Lee

We were in Andrew and Elizabeth's sitting room. I had been plied with hot, sweet tea, good for shock, they had informed me. Everyone else appeared to be on the brandy!

DCI Hutton stood facing us, Christopher, Paul and I were on the large, plush sofa, Andrew and Elizabeth in two of the armchairs.

Joseph was noticeably absent, he was still being held at the police station pending enquiries.

'How are you feeling now?' the inspector asked, 'I think we should get you to A&E to get you checked out.'

I put my hand to my forehead. Elizabeth had done some first aid on the injuries I'd sustained when I hit my head and shoulder on the balcony rails as I fell to its floor. I could vaguely remember the feeling of lightness, as Flynn and Kelsey were dragged off me by Hutton and Paul.

'Later,' I said, 'I want to hear what put you onto Flynn and Kelsey. I need answers.'

The inspector coughed, 'Well, nothing made sense if you looked at the events separately, but put together, there could only be one solution. Let's start with Joseph. As we all know now, he was baby farming, but he wasn't acting alone. He was working alongside two other people, Freddie Emmerson and a doctor by the name of Richard Wyatt.'

'Flynn's father,' I said, 'He told me his parents were both medics.'

Hutton continued his narrative, 'Yes, Flynn's father

worked at the Helen Rosewell Maternity Home. I first suspected that one of his partners might have been you, Andrew. My apologies for that. But to go on, Flynn, Mark, Christopher, Kelsey and Shannon were friends from a very young age, although Kelsey wasn't as close to the group as the others were, and only really became part of their little clique after they all grew up.

'She then began seeing Flynn Wyatt, and at some stage they discovered they had an interest in common. They both wanted Joseph Chase's blood!

'Flynn, because Joseph had been as much involved in the baby scam as his father, but had let his father shoulder all the blame. Richard Wyatt had tried to take Joseph down with him, but Joseph had a lot of clout with the authorities back then, and because of his position, Wyatt's claims were never checked out. That would certainly not happen today!

'Freddie Emmerson pleaded guilty, but was let off with a fine and a warning, as he'd already left the baby farming ring, declaring it to be against his principles, and on the grounds that he had a mentally ill wife and young daughter to care for.'

'So this was the trouble you were referring to, Mrs Colbourne,' Paul said.

She nodded, 'I never had proof, but yes, I suspected he was involved in something illegal, now I know exactly what!'

'So now we come to Kelsey,' said the inspector, 'She only learned of her father's involvement shortly before her mother died, when Dorothy Emmerson told her that Joseph was the cause of all her problems. If she and Freddie hadn't been dragged into it by Joseph, Dorothy wouldn't have felt the guilt and fear of discovery all those years. Dorothy was the nurse Wyatt brought in to care for the sick babies, although she was never a qualified nurse at all. But that didn't matter, she was not there to tend the sick. All the babies in her care were healthy and waiting to be farmed out to new parents. Dorothy was known as Dotty back then, and as she had nothing to do with the hospital before the scam no one knew any different.

'Freddie moved his family to Dengate, hoping for a fresh start, but when Dorothy found out that Joseph was also here, her condition rapidly deteriorated, ending in her taking her own life by swallowing half a bottle of sleeping tablets. So of course, Kelsey blamed Joseph for her mother's death. She also believed he was trying to ruin her father's business, there had always been rivalry between he two firms, but despite this, they had occasionally worked together on projects beneficial to both companies. So Kelsey tried to turn the tables and play Joseph at his own game by ruining his company. To her it was a power game. That's when she made a play for Christopher.'

'So she was just using me all the time,' Chris said dejectedly.

'I'm afraid so,' Hutton replied, 'She saw you as a way in to Chase/Colbourne.'

'She was pushing me, inspector,' Chris said, 'Pushing me to get to the top and get some control over the board. Then she was planning to step in and bring the company down.' He paused, 'It was me who leaked Joseph's story to the press. I'm not making excuses for myself, I know it was wrong, and I take full responsibility for what I've done, but I'd never have thought of doing something like that if it hadn't been for her pushing me. But just for the record, I didn't have anything to do with Mark or Eve Pritchard's murders. I'd draw the line at that!'

Hutton was glad Christopher appeared to be showing some remorse, Kelsey was a difficult woman to say no to, especially if you were totally besotted with her as Chris had been.

'So they murdered Eve to stop her talking,' the inspector went on, 'Shannon had been giving Eve lessons in Italian, and Eve in return had taught Shannon to play the piano. The two had become very close before Shannon's accident, that's why she was so sure who you were.' This last statement was directed at me.

'Either Flynn or Kelsey must have been in town that day and heard every word that passed between you,' the inspector continued.

'It was Flynn,' I reflected, 'He helped me retrieve my car keys from a grid where I'd dropped them'

I turned to Christopher, 'Flynn used me every bit as much as Kelsey used you.' I could see now he'd only befriended me as a means to keeping tabs on me. It was always his plan to take me out if I got too close to the truth.

'It was also Flynn that murdered Eve,' I said, remembering how long he'd taken to supposedly get his wallet out of the car. And how Kelsey had kept Yvonne Whitmore, the fortune teller, talking until Flynn had reappeared from the tent.'

I looked at Inspector Hutton, 'Was it also Flynn who sent those anonymous letters all along then?'

I was prepared to believe anything of him now!

'I think Elizabeth can answer that,' Hutton said, glancing at Elizabeth, who was shuffling about uncomfortably in her chair.

She looked across at me, 'I sent them, Lee. But not to threaten you. I foresaw trouble the first time I saw you, looking the image of Shannon. I just thought to get you away from here as quickly as possible. I'm sorry, I know it was the wrong way to go about things, but at the time I thought it was Christopher who was responsible for all this. Joseph had severed all ties with him and I thought there must be a good reason for that. I suspected Joseph thought it was all down to Chris too, but of course he couldn't go to the police as the whole story about the baby farming thing would have come out. I hope you'll forgive me, Lee. I only wanted to protect you.'

I smiled at her, 'I understand, but if you knew me

better, you'd know I would never be frightened away. It just made me more determined to get to the bottom of what was going on.'

'Shannon would have done the same thing,' she said quietly.

I turned back to Inspector Hutton, 'One thing I still don't understand is why I had those flashbacks that belonged to my sister. The last one was really vivid. I knew for sure it was Flynn and Kelsey on that balcony that night. I saw them looking down at me just before I blacked out. Why did Shannon have to die? Couldn't they have found a way to bring Joseph's company down without resorting to murder?'

Hutton looked around the room, he had a captive audience, 'Mark and Shannon were the direct heirs to Joseph's fortune, and also the company. So when you came back, Flynn and Kelsey knew they had to get rid of you quickly, because they were the only two people who knew the complete truth. They realised they hadn't done a good enough job the first time. You didn't die when you were supposed to, but they felt a bit safer when it became apparent that you had no memory of anything that happened before they sent you over that balcony. Those flashbacks were not your sister's memories. They were your own.'

It slowly dawned on me what he was saying. I looked him in the eye, and took a deep breath.

'So I really am Shannon after all!'

It was a lot to take in. The flashbacks were my own memories, I was Shannon Chase, and Joseph was my adoptive father. My mind went back to the portrait in his bedroom. My mother. No wonder I was drawn to it. Snatches of memory were flashing through my mind, a mother and daughter playing tennis on the court in the garden of the Manchester house, cycle rides along country lanes, picnics in the meadows. The memories were faint, but they were there!

I was suddenly transported out of my reverie by an uncomfortable thought.

'Inspector, if I'm Shannon, and it was me they pulled out of that wrecked car, what happened to the real Lee?'

Chapter 24

Four years earlier

Amelia Stafford glanced across the room to where Flynn Wyatt was sitting with that awful Kelsey Emmerson. Why did he have to bring her along? Amelia hadn't invited her, she'd just turned up with Flynn, holding on to his arm as if to say, 'Hands off, he's mine!'

She looked at the other people gathered round Flynn's table. Shannon Chase, Mark Colbourne, his new girlfriend, Jo, and Christopher Chase, Shannon's cousin. Flynn had been part of that group for as long as Amelia could remember, but to get him to attend her 21st birthday party, she had to invite the whole group.

Not that she minded that much. Shannon and Mark were okay, Christopher was a bit of a drip at times, and she had known Joanna Parsons since her schooldays.

The music was loud, the food good. And of course, there was plenty of drink. She watched Shannon and Chris select a few snacks from the buffet, and wished she felt hungry enough to eat some herself, but she couldn't get her mind off that girl drooling all over Flynn!

Jo wasn't eating either. She was on one of her many diets, Amelia wondered why she bothered. Jo had a great figure, she was slim and attractive. She and Mark Colbourne looked good together.

Amelia's eyes followed Flynn and Kelsey, who were dancing now, his arms around her in just the way Amelia wished he would hold her.

Kelsey lifted her face for a kiss, and Amelia looked away. This was not how she had envisaged things would go. She glanced at the clock on the wall, 11.15. At midnight the party would be over, and suddenly Amelia couldn't wait.

Shannon, having finished her snack was dancing with Chris, Amelia watched as they glided round the floor. Amelia wondered why Shannon didn't have a boyfriend. Surely she didn't fancy her cousin!

The dance ended and the little group collected their belongings and left. Amelia felt like crying. They hadn't even stayed till the end! The evening had been a disaster.

'What do you say we carry this on somewhere else?' Flynn said, as they got outside into the sultry air.

'Sounds good,' Chris replied, 'You got somewhere in mind?'

Flynn looked at Kelsey, who was swigging from a bottle of wine as she walked.

'Your grandmother's place is empty at the moment. How about going there?' Flynn suggested.

Kelsey was silent for a moment, then, 'Perfect! I have a key. Hilltops here we come!'

She marched off down the road, more than a little drunk. The others followed.

It had been a hot, humid day, but now the dark clouds began gathering overhead. Shannon looked up, 'We'll have to hurry, I don't fancy getting a soaking tonight.'

Hilltops was not far from the hall where Amelia's party had been held. It was a large, retro styled building, with large windows divided into the oblong sections of that period.

'Should we have asked Amelia to come along?' asked Chris.

'What the hell for?' Kelsey turned round, after taking another swig from the bottle, 'She's the biggest drip out!'

Flynn grinned, privately he agreed with her. He wasn't sure why they'd all been invited in the first place, unless it was Amelia's connection with Jo.

The house was in darkness when they arrived and Kelsey fumbled around in her bag for the key, finally unlocking the door and stepping inside. 'Welcome to my humble abode,' she laughed.

'It's not your abode, it's your grandmother's,' Chris corrected her. Kelsey ignored him.

'Where's the bloody light switch?' Flynn said, feeling his way along the wall. Kelsey sauntered over to him and switched on the light. The others looked around, they were in a chintzy, flowery sitting room.

'Very old lady!' Chris said, turning up his nose at the floral furnishings.

'You're drunk!' Kelsey told him.

'You can talk!' he replied, crouching down and opening the door of the drinks cabinet.

'Cherry brandy, Ooh, la la, very posh!'

Kelsey crossed the room and slapped him across the back of the head, 'Feel free to leave any time soon!' she said, with venom in her voice.

Chris carried on examining the contents of the drinks cabinet until he found what he was looking for. 'Ah, this is better,' he said, taking out an unopened bottle of whisky, unscrewing the top and taking a long swig.

The others ignored him and he carried on drinking until Mark snatched the bottle from his hand,'You've had enough.'

Chris looked daggers at him, but staggered outside and sat down on the doorstep. He was out cold in minutes.

'I think we'll call it a night,' Mark told the others. Joanna looked relieved. She hadn't wanted to come here after they'd left the party, but her romance with Mark was new, and these were his friends, she didn't want to argue with him at this stage, so she'd just gone along with it.

Flynn tossed his car keys at Mark, 'Just bring my car up here before you go, will you? You haven't had as much booze as the rest of us.'

They had all left their cars at the hall. Mark nodded, and he and Jo left to walk the short distance down the hill. About twenty minutes later, they heard him park the car outside the house and push the keys through the letter box.

Flynn and Kelsey looked at each other. They heard Mark and Jo's footsteps crunching on the gravel as they walked down the drive for the second time that evening.

There was just Flynn, Kelsey and Shannon left now, Chris was still flaked out on the front porch.

'I feel a bit, woozy,' Shannon remarked, 'I think I'll call a taxi.'

Flynn had been plying her with drinks all evening, 'You just need to lay down for a bit. She can crash on your gran's bed for a while, cant she?' he asked Kelsey.

'Sure. Follow me.' Kelsey marched off into the hall, Flynn and Shannon following her. At the top of the stairs, she led them into a bedroom and opened the French windows that led onto the balcony. She stepped out into the sultry night air.

'Fresh air. That's what you need,' Flynn led Shannon out, gripping her arm tightly. The railings round the balcony were black wrought iron, with a wide ledge around the top.

Shannon took a few deep breaths, taking as much oxygen into her lungs as she could.

'Better?' asked Flynn.

She nodded, watching Kelsey, who was running her fingers backwards and forwards along the ledge.

'Remember when we were kids and you used to climb up and walk right round the ledge?'

Flynn nodded.

'I wonder if you could still do it?' Kelsey challenged him.

'Don't be bloody funny, Kelsey. I didn't know any better as a kid. I'm not that stupid now.'

Shannon listened to their banter, wondering what was

going on. Kelsey hadn't been part of their group as a kid. And this was her grandmother's house, Flynn wouldn't have even been here as a child!

Flynn suddenly let go of her arm and climbed up on the ledge. Shannon looked on in horror, but Kelsey was smiling. They watched him take the first tentative steps, arms outstretched for balance as he slowly walked along the top of the railings, then jumped off at the other end, landing safely inside the perimeter of the balcony.

Kelsey made a whooping sound and Shannon edged back towards the French windows. She could make a run for it then. They'd probably catch up with her, but at least she'd be away from the balcony. She had always been nervous of heights, and this stupid act of bravado on Flynn's part wasn't helping.

'Your turn, Kelsey,' Flynn was saying.

She laughed, 'Too drunk. I'm seeing two of everything now! I wouldn't know which ledge to put my feet on! How about you Shannon? You haven't had as much booze as I have. Make her do it, Flynn.'

She took another swig from the bottle, and Flynn grabbed hold of Shannon, dragging her towards the ledge. 'It's wider than it looks,' he said quietly, 'Have a go, just to appease her. Then I'll get you out of here.'

Shannon struggled to free herself from his grip, but he just held on to her tighter.

'Let me go, Flynn. The party's over. If you want to do everything she asks that's fine, but I'm going home.'

His face changed, and Shannon suddenly felt afraid of him. She had never seen this side of Flynn before. 'I don't think so,' he said, and with a quick movement, scooped her up in his arms and sat her on the ledge, her back to the openness that was beckoning behind her.

'Let me go, Flynn, this isn't funny.'

'It is from where I'm standing,' Kelsey smirked, slowly walking towards where Shannon was precariously perched.

'You're sick!' Shannon watched as the girl's beautiful face turned evil.

Kelsey stood, legs akimbo, just staring into space. 'The sins of the father,' she said, her voice almost a whisper. Then she seemed to snap out of her trance and yelled, 'Now, Flynn. Do it now!'

He hesitated only a moment, and then with both hands pushed Shannon backwards over the balcony.

They both stepped forward and peered over the edge.

'One down, one to go,' Kelsey looked round at Flynn, suddenly not so drunk any more.

Flynn had sobered up too, enough to speak rationally. 'No rush, Kelsey. We can't touch Mark for a while. It would look suspicious, both the heirs to Chase/Colbourne having fatal accidents at the same time. Leave it with me. I'll know when the time is right.'

They went back through the bedroom, closing the French windows behind them. 'We've got to get her away from here. This is my grandmother's house, we're not even supposed to be here. I had to nick the key out of my dad's bureau,' Kelsey said, as they went downstairs switching the lights off and locking the front door as they went. Chris was sprawled across the porch, totally oblivious to what had just happened.

Flynn kicked the sole of Chris's shoe a couple of times. Chris growled, but stayed unconscious.

'He'll be out for a while,' Flynn said, grabbing Kelsey's hand and hurrying to where Shannon lay prone beneath the balcony.

Kelsey took one look at Shannon's injuries and started gagging. Flynn took her firmly by the shoulders and gently shook her. 'This is not the time to decide you have a phobia of blood,' he said firmly, though he had to swallow down the bile that was rising in his own throat, 'Now take a deep breath and pull yourself together. We have to get her out of here before Chris wakes up.' He lifted Shannon under her shoulders and instructed Kelsey to take her feet. Together, they started to carry her towards the car. 'What was that?' Kelsey whispered, on hearing a movement from the front of the house.

Flynn had heard it too, and stopped dead in his tracks, 'Chris! He's woken up. We mustn't make a sound or he'll see us.'

They stood there, half hidden by the foliage, not moving a muscle. Shannon was beginning to weigh heavy, Kelsey was afraid she was going to drop her.

Chris had scrambled up and was staggering down the path singing, 'Oh, what a beautiful morning, hic!' Then he vomited into the bushes!

'Ugh!' Kelsey whispered, 'That's disgusting. I can smell it from here!' She began gagging and received a glare from Flynn, 'If you're gonna puke for God's sake do it quietly!' he whispered back.

Kelsey took a few deep breaths and got control of herself.

Flynn shook his head in disbelief, he'd been sure Chris would be out for at least another half an hour.

'Okay, let's go,' he said, 'But quietly in case he turns round and comes back.'

'Why would he do that?' Kelsey hissed, wondering how much further the car was.

'He's completely disorientated, you saw the way he staggered down the path. He could be going round in circles all night.'

'He's not safe to drive,' Kelsey whispered, 'Suppose he has an accident on the way home?'

'Kelsey, we've just killed a young woman, and you're worrying about a drunken idiot who means absolutely nothing to you?'

'He's not a threat to us. His father hasn't done anything to hurt us, hers has!' She gestured to Shannon, then looked away quickly. 'I didn't think the fall would make this much mess! We should have used poison.'

'Then we couldn't pass it off as an accident. I've been

plying Shannon with booze all evening, there's bound to still be some in her bloodstream in the morning. This way it's plausible that she wandered out onto the balcony, got disorientated and took a fall over the edge.'

They reached the car and Flynn laid a tartan rug over the back seat and laid Shannon on it. 'I'll dispose of the rug, it's bound to get blood on it somewhere' Flynn said, as they got into the car.

'Blood stains! What if there's blood on the ground where she fell?'

Flynn got out of the car, 'Wait here. I'll sort it.'

Kelsey wasn't happy at being left alone with a blood-soaked body, but took some deep breaths and tried to relax. Shannon was dead, wasn't she? There was nothing she could do to hurt her now.

Flynn came back about ten minutes later, 'I got some water out of the butt, and washed the patio down as best I could. If I've missed anything, there's going to be a storm, so the rain will do the rest, and your grandmother doesn't get back from her cruise for another three weeks. No one's going to check out her place when Shannon is going to be found under her own window.'

The rain started falling as they drove along, first lightly, then it turned heavier, lashing against the windscreen, the wipers struggling to keep the screen clear. A rumble of thunder could be heard in the distance.

Flynn put his foot down, washing the patio down hadn't been on his agenda, and he was anxious to get Shannon back to her father's house before the storm built.

Suddenly there was a flash of headlights coming towards them, and then things seemed to happen in slow motion. Flynn swerved to avoid the oncoming car, which seemed to be heading straight for him. He slammed on the brakes and the car skidded across the road and then screeched to a stop. He watched in horror as the other car skidded off the wet, slippery road and turned on its side in a field.

'Bloody Hell!' said Kelsey, adjusting herself after being shot forward in her seat, 'We can't stop, Flynn, We've got a dead body on the back seat. What if the police come along!' she screamed hysterically. This was all going wrong! They'd got so close and now some idiot on the road threatened to ruin it all by causing a traffic accident, 'Flynn! Just drive! Lets get out of here!'

'Stay here,' Flynn yelled at her as he got out of the car. He ran towards the wreck of the other car and peered inside. Two minutes later he was back, soaking wet, but incredulous, 'You're not going to believe this. There's a dead girl in that car, the spitting image of Shannon. They could be twins!'

There was a movement from the back of the car, followed by a low groan. Then silence.

'She's not dead!' Kelsey cried, 'What are we going to do!'

'Damn!' said Flynn, 'I have an idea, but I need you to stay calm. We're going to put Shannon in that car, and take her double back to Joseph's house. I'm going to back up to the other car and then you're going to help me lift Shannon out of this one. This will work, but we have to be quick. Do you understand?'

Kelsey nodded, 'What if Shannon wakes up and tells them who she really is?' she asked.

'Have you seen her injuries?' Flynn asked, sarcastically, 'She can't last much longer, and if she does her brain is going to be mush!'

Kelsey nodded, trying to convince herself of this. Flynn started the engine and slowly backed up as near to the other car as he possibly could. 'So far, so good' he grinned at Kelsey.

The rain was easing, making their task slightly easier. They lifted the dead girl from the car and carefully laid her on the ground while they placed Shannon in the other car, in exactly the same position her double had been in. There was no doubt that the other girl was dead, they'd have to take their chances on Shannon surviving, but the odds were against it. There was no time to do anything about it now, someone could come along at any minute.

With Shannon's double now lying on the back seat, they hit the road again, this time slower and more carefully. The rain had diminished to a light drizzle, the storm having passed over.

'Those people in the front of the car,' Kelsey said, her voice calm again, 'They'll know she's not their daughter.'

'Both dead,' Flynn said, bluntly. 'You know Shannon was adopted?'

'Of course,' Kelsey replied, 'Are you suggesting those people in that car could have been her birth parents? That would mean the girl we've got in our car is Shannon's sister. And we meet them on a wet, stormy night, on a deserted road, just when we need somewhere to offload Shannon? Incredible! What are the chances of that happening?'

'The odds are pretty remote. But that's exactly what has happened. I couldn't believe it when I looked in that car, I'd left Shannon in our car, yet there she was in the car of complete strangers! I think they're not just sisters. I think they're identical twins.' he said, with a grin, 'Just how lucky can you get!'

They passed Chris, weaving his way over both sides of the road, but at least he was heading in the right direction.

'We'll have to be quick,' said Flynn, 'It won't take him more than about twenty minutes to walk the rest of the way.'

'Do you think he noticed our car?' Kelsey asked.

'The state he's in, I doubt if he'd notice if it ran right over him! But I think its best if we don't let on that we were in your grandmother's house. I think I cleaned things up okay, but I wouldn't want anyone snooping about there. If anybody asks, we left the party shortly after Mark and Jo. Chris was out cold. No one can say different. But I'll have a word with him and tell him we were at the cottage illicitly, and you don't want a backlashing from your dad I don't think anyone will catch on that 'Shannon' died anywhere but at her own home, but we have to cover all possibilities.'

'And Mark?' Kelsey asked, wanting be sure everyone would be telling the same story.

'He won't say anything, but if it makes you happy I'll speak to him too.'

'What about the vomit Chris kindly left my gran as a welcome home present?'

'It doesn't stain like blood. And it'll be long gone before your gran comes home. The heavy rain we had tonight will have helped. Now stop panicking, we're almost home and dry.'

'What about Shannon's car? It's still at the hall. How are we going to explain how she got home?'

'She could have got a taxi, thumbed a lift, walked. She'd have done it a damn sight quicker than Chris! Don't worry, it's going to be fine.'

They parked the car just outside Joseph's driveway, carried the dead girl quickly and quietly through the garden, and placed her under the balcony, positioning her as if she'd just fallen.

Then they hurried back to their car and drove away. There was no sign of Chris. He was still staggering about somewhere on the road, to arrive five minutes later to find his cousin dead from a fall from her balcony. Kelsey reached for a tissue to wipe her face, she wasn't sure if it was the drizzle or her own sweat making her feel uncomfortable. They had cut things a bit fine, but the stress she had felt earlier was gradually evaporating.

She looked at the time on the dashboard, 2.34, nice timing. She sat back and relaxed, a smile on her face. They had done it!

Several miles away, on a quiet road just outside

Manchester, Jason Webb was pulling 'Lee Filmer' out of the wreckage of a car.

Chapter 25

Shannon

Paul and I were painting the rest of the cottage. I was not now going to change the kitchen units or the bathroom suite. What was the point when I was going to put the place up for sale? I had notified Aunt Millicent's solicitor as soon as I'd found out I was not Lee, the rightful inheritor of the property, but after reviewing the situation he decided that as Lee was now deceased, I, as her twin sister would become her rightful heir.

He changed the names on the deeds from Lee Filmer to Shannon Chase. So now I just needed to smarten the place up a bit before putting it on the market.

'Are you sure you don't want to stay here?' Paul had asked.

I had given it some serious thought, but it had too many bad memories for me. The only good thing was that I'd met Paul.

My adoptive father, Joseph Chase, had a heart attack just after his arrest for the baby farming episode. He was not expected to live long, and I was not sure I could forgive him for what he'd done to my real family.

It was better if I just left Barling altogether, make a fresh start somewhere else. I'd come here looking for memories, but most of what I'd learned I'd be more than happy to forget! I had promised to stay in touch with Elizabeth and Andrew though. Elizabeth promised to send me the portrait of the lady I had always known as my mother, once Joseph had passed away. Isla had known about how they had become parents to me, but had been ignorant of Joseph's further involvement with the maternity home, and had always had my best interest at heart. The fleeting memories I had of her were fond ones.

Chris seemed to have got very friendly with Joanna just lately. I wondered if anything would come of that.

As for the company, as Joseph's heir, I was set to inherit his side of that too. But I didn't want it. It had been partly financed with dirty money, as was Emmerson's business, and I was happy to hand any shares I would inherit over to Chris. Now he was out of Kelsey's clutches, I felt sure he'd do an excellent job of running the company.

Since the night Flynn and Kelsey had tried to kill me, I'd had brief flashes of memory. If this was as good as it gets, it was okay with me, I now had a past and more importantly, a future.

The 'For Sale' sign went up on the cottage on the day Paul told me he had been offered a promotion, but it would mean moving to the Bournemouth area. He asked me to go with him, and of course I said yes.

So all I had to do now was wait for the cottage to be sold.

Paul and I left for Bournemouth on the day Flynn and Kelsey were convicted for murder. As Kelsey herself had once told me, you reap what you sow!

THE END

Also by Teresa Colton:

Mirror Image

Two young girls believe they are being stalked, and the police don't seem to be taking them seriously. Then a hostess from a local nightclub us found murdered, and the girls are convinced it is the work of their stalker.

Inspector Hutton leads his first murder case. He has plenty of suspects, but none with an apparent motive. And who is the mysterious Alice? Can he track down the killer before he strikes again? And are the girls really in danger?

Printed in Poland
by Amazon Fulfillment
Poland Sp. z o.o., Wrocław